"So much for taking Lon— "Are you ready to give up and come home?"

She knew he was teasing, but she refused to give in anyway. "Never!" she declared vehemently. "I still have to convince Mother that I'm an adult. Do you know she refused to let the musicians play a waltz when I asked?"

"Horrors!" Geoffrey cried in mock dismay, enjoying the fire in her eye and the way she jutted out her chin defiantly. "A little too wicked for the proper London family, eh?"

Allison tossed her head. "Everyone who is anyone dances the waltz. Lady Jersey says so!"

"Really?" He couldn't let such a moment pass. He stripped off his coat, tossing it on the table. "I surely wouldn't want this evening to be a total disappointment for you. By all means, let us waltz."

Allison stared at him, sure he was still teasing. He held out his arms encouragingly. She looked dubious. "You cannot be serious."

"Why not? This is one place your mother will surely not invade tonight. And we'd better be quick about it or the servants will invade. That supper will not last forever." He sketched a bow, lowering his head so she would not see the hope in his eyes. "Miss Munroe, may I have the honor of this dance?"

Her laugh bubbled up, spoiling the seriousness of her answering curtsey. "Mr. Pentercast, I would be delighted."

He slipped his arms about her slender waist. Humming, he led her about the room in what he hoped was something approaching the dance he had only seen performed once before.

Allison's heart was beating much faster than the slow, careful movements would imply. She didn't want to think why. This was far more fun than the ball, and not a little frightening, if in a heady sort of way. Geoffrey's gaze was warm and soft, bathing her in appreciation and pleasure. She could have danced like this the entire night. . . .

Books by Regina Scott

THE UNFLAPPABLE MISS FAIRCHILD
THE TWELVE DAYS OF CHRISTMAS
THE BLUESTOCKING ON HIS KNEE
CATCH OF THE SEASON

Published by Zebra Books

CATCH OF
THE SEASON

REGINA SCOTT

Zebra Books
Kensington Publishing Corp.

http://www.zebrabooks.com

ZEBRA BOOKS are published by

Kensington Publishing Corp.
850 Third Avenue
New York, NY 10022

Copyright © 1999 by Regina Lundgren

All rights reserved. No part of this book may be reproduced in any form or by any means without the prior written consent of the Publisher, excepting brief quotes used in reviews.

If you purchased this book without a cover you should be aware that this book is stolen property. It was reported as "unsold and destroyed" to the Publisher and neither the Author nor the Publisher has received any payment for this "stripped book."

Zebra and the Z logo Reg. U.S. Pat. & TM Off.

First Printing: October, 1999
10 9 8 7 6 5 4 3 2 1

Printed in the United States of America

To my brother, Rick Brown, who has Enoch's temperament and Geoffrey's enthusiasm. May he someday find the perfect girl for him.

Prologue

Mayfair, London
Near the Start of the Season, 1813

Allison Munroe had no idea that her fate was being sealed. She had concerns of her own as she accompanied her sister Genevieve shopping for gloves to match the gown Gen was to wear to Allison's come-out ball. She was having a difficult time looking forward to the event, when only three months before she had been anxiously awaiting it. And even though she was ready to admit that her change in attitude was closely connected to a certain young man, marriage was the farthest thing from Allison's mind. She had only the faintest of premonitions that it might be on the Marquis DeGuis's mind. Of course, that was exactly what the marquis had intended when he had sent the note to her mother a few days previously. He considered it highly improper for the young lady to know his intentions before her parents did, and the marquis was never improper.

"I must meet with you on a matter of some importance," the carefully worded note had read. "It concerns your daughter's future happiness. Please return word of a time when we might meet in private. Sincerely yours, Thomas, Marquis DeGuis."

The widow Munroe was certain she knew what the

important matter was. While Allison seemed oblivious, her mother thought the marquis had been rather marked in his attentions to Allison since their arrival in London two months ago. She hadn't wanted to attribute too much to the drives in the park or the occasional afternoon call, but when he had asked Allison to dance three times at Grace Dunsworthy's come-out ball last week, Mrs. Munroe was sure he had made his intentions clear.

Ermintrude Munroe's gray-blue eyes gazed off into space as she sat waiting for the marquis in the sunny sitting room of the London town house they had rented for the Season. She still could not credit how her daughter could have attracted such a man as the marquis. Dashing, wealthy, and titled, he was one of the most sought-after bachelors on the marriage mart that year.

Allison was lovely; there was no doubt about that. Unfortunately, she was nearly as tall as most of the men of the *ton*. Thankfully, the fact that she tended to look the men boldly in their eyes did not seem to bother them as much as her mother had feared. But to her mother's mind, Allison had a regrettable tendency to speak without thinking . . . and rather loudly at that. Her lanky figure made her a tolerable dancer and an excellent horsewoman, but her grace when moving about a withdrawing room or taking dinner with company left something to be desired. Mrs. Munroe hoped her daughter hadn't mentioned that she kept a pet ferret with an annoying habit of escaping at exactly the right moment to create total chaos in a social situation. And, of course, the marquis wouldn't have had time to learn that her embroidery consisted of knots and ill-placed threads; that the only words she had mastered in French were those no well-bred young lady should claim to know; and that, if left to her own devices, her choice in reading material could only be called original.

Mrs. Munroe certainly hoped that the marquis was willing to overlook such deficits and focus on Allison's one shining trait: her kind heart. Allison was considerate with everyone, and with those in need most of all. Furthermore, once she had made a friend, Allison was loyal to the point of obsession.

Look at how she had practically adopted that oaf Geoffrey Pentercast last Christmas when all the world thought him the veriest villain. As it turned out, he was as innocent as Allison had claimed him to be, but that was beside the point. Another young lady of their circle, Mrs. Munroe was sure, would have had nothing to do with him after he had been accused of being the village vandal. But Allison had ever followed her own heart. It was her mother's duty to make sure that when it came to something as important as choosing a marriage partner, the choice was made with more thought than someone as young, loyal, and heedless as Allison could provide.

She heard the sound of the door knocker and absently patted an iron-gray hair back into place. Another woman might have glanced about the small, satin-draped room to make sure the servants had dusted the correctly placed collection of Chippendale armchairs and matching sofa, knowing the man she was about to entertain had a reputation for being fastidious. But Ermintrude Munroe was nothing if not fastidious herself, and no room she had owned had ever not been properly dusted.

Another woman might have paused to wonder whether the floral-patterned walls, upholstery, and Aubusson carpet were perhaps too obvious for a gentleman who was known to pride himself on his subtlety. However, the widow Munroe considered the soft roses and ivories and the cool blues the perfect choice to tone down the sunlight coming through the gauze curtains. The whole decor gave the room a gentle feeling of femininity that satisfied her as an appropriate place in which to discuss marriage.

Another woman would have at least sat a little straighter in the scroll-backed armchair, knowing she was soon to be in the presence of the aristocracy, but Ermintrude Munroe was already sitting ramrod straight. She had her own reputation to maintain, the reputation of keeping her poise in the face of the most dire calamity. An event as minor as an interview with a prospective son-in-law was hardly enough to cause so much as a tremor. Her classic features were composed, her lavender silk day dress showed nary a crease. She was the epitome of refined womanhood, and that was exactly what the marquis noted with approval as he entered.

"The Marquis DeGuis, madame," Perkins intoned with a bow of his equally ramrod-straight back. Hiding a smile of satisfaction, Mrs. Munroe inclined her head in recognition of the peer. Even though she had hired Perkins only for the Season, she was seriously considering taking him back with her to Wenwood Abbey, their home in Somerset. A butler, she had always felt, should reflect the good taste and refinement of his employers. One simply could not find fault in Perkins's dignified tread, his spotless black coat and knee breeches, or his noble profile. The marquis, of course, did not indicate that he noticed what a paragon of servitude Perkins was, but that was only to be expected.

"Mrs. Munroe," Lord DeGuis murmured, moving to take her hand and bow over it. "Thank you for receiving me."

"Always a pleasure, sir," Mrs. Munroe assured him, noting that Perkins had taken up his place to one side of the doorway and stood as silent and immobile as a

Grecian statue. "Please." She nodded to the marquis. "Won't you sit down?"

"Thank you," the marquis replied, seating himself on a chair not far from her. It gave her a moment to appreciate the precise cut of his short raven hair, the sapphire gaze, and the composed, chiseled features of his handsome face. It also gave her a moment to note with approval the perfect cut of his immaculate navy coat and fawn-colored trousers. They could only have been done by Weston. He was every bit as polished and refined as she had first thought. And every bit too refined and polished for a young hoyden like her Allison. She wondered again whether she could have misinterpreted his motives.

"And how are all the Munroes?" the marquis asked dutifully, diamond stickpin glinting from the folds of his perfectly but elaborately tied cravat. "I understand from Miss Munroe that her sister has been unwell."

Mrs. Munroe let the tiniest of sighs escape. "Yes, she was, but we are all in satisfactory health now. Thank you for asking. I think it was only the rich London food that upset Genevieve's constitution for a time. She is used to the plainer fare one generally gets in the country."

"Quite understandable," the marquis agreed. "And how is Miss Munroe enjoying her sojourn in London?"

"Very nicely, thank you," she replied. "She is at this moment out shopping with her sister for the come-out ball," she added, hoping to assure him that they would not be disturbed, if he were indeed going to ask something of a personal nature. "She is quite looking forward to it, as you might imagine."

"As am I," the marquis assured her. He eyed her for a moment thoughtfully, then straightened his broad shoulders. "Mrs. Munroe, might I speak candidly?"

"Certainly," Mrs. Munroe granted him. "You and my

daughter seem to have become friends. I hope you can speak to me as you would to her."

He smiled. "Well, perhaps not entirely. Your daughter is remarkably quiet in my presence."

Mrs. Munroe struggled not to show her surprise. "Indeed?"

"Indeed. I find her delightful in that regard. So many young ladies deem it witty to prattle on about the most nonsensical things. Your daughter has the great virtue of knowing when to remain silent. In fact, Mrs. Munroe, your daughter is quite the most perfect specimen of womanhood I have had the pleasure of meeting."

The man was obviously besotted; there was no other way to explain his assessment. Allison, remaining silent? She could not imagine how he had gotten that impression. She had never known Allison to remain silent above a moment. "Of course it does a mother's heart good to hear her daughter praised, sir," she managed.

"Who could not praise her? She is lovely, unassuming, and the most docile of creatures. Yet she dances and rides with a spirit few can show. In short, Mrs. Munroe, I find that your daughter would make an excellent marchioness. What can I say or do that would convince you to grant me her hand in marriage?"

It was one of the few times in her life that Ermintrude Munroe was ever tempted to leap to her feet and shout for joy. Instead, she forced herself to remember her duty to her daughter. If Allison had somehow managed to attach him, Mrs. Munroe must do nothing that might cause him to have second thoughts.

"I am aware of your family connections, my lord," she replied with the proper deference. "It is well known that the DeGuis are descended from the Normans. Your excellent reputation for handling your estates procedes you as well. Having seen you with my daughter, I can safely say that you would make her an excellent husband. Have you mentioned your feelings to Allison?"

The marquis sat even straighter, blue eyes flashing. "Certainly not! It would be most improper of me to speak to Miss Munroe without speaking to you first."

Mrs. Munroe inclined her head in acknowledgment, pleased by his response. "Of course. Forgive me. I am very glad to hear that you feel as I do about the proper course of matters. A decision about marriage is better made with more experienced heads than my daughter's."

"Then I can count on your support?"

Mrs. Munroe held up her hand, making sure he listened as she stated her case. "In general, sir, you may. You have my permission to marry my daughter. However, as I'm sure you will understand, this Season is very important to her. It will properly introduce her to Society. It will allow her to meet a number of young ladies she may count on as friends in the future. And it will give her the social polish you will need her to have as your marchioness. She will do much better if you do not announce your engagement until the end of the Season."

The marquis frowned. "But if she does not know she is engaged to me, she may form an attachment to some other fellow."

"My dear marquis"—Mrs. Munroe smiled indulgently—"as long as you dance attendance, what young lady could possibly look elsewhere?"

The marquis's frown turned into a satisfied smile. "Very well. I can understand what this Season must mean to Miss Munroe. As long as I have your solemn word that your daughter's hand is mine within the year, I will remain silent for now."

Mrs. Munroe offered him her hand, and he bowed

over it again. "My lord, you have my word. Allison will be your bride before Parliament starts in November. You will be a most welcome addition to the family."

One

Allison Munroe was finally to have her long-anticipated come out. She had begged and pleaded and yearned for the day for the last four years, ever since her fourteenth birthday. She had dreamed of wearing her blond hair high and her slender neckline low. She had envisioned the elegant dancing couples, the delectable foods, and the splendid conversation so many times that she often wondered whether they hadn't already occurred. Now the much-hoped-for event was in reality only a week away.

And she could hardly wait to get it over with.

She found it hard to understand her change in attitude. She had been looking forward to the event right up until the time she left Wenwood Abbey. She could not see how the journey of a little over a hundred miles could so change her. It wasn't that by traveling she had lost family or friends to witness her moment of glory. Her mother and older sister Genevieve had accompanied her, and ever since she had arrived in London in March, she had met any number of young ladies from sixteen to nineteen who would be making their debuts this Season. Some seemed almost competitive about the whole affair, which seemed rather pointless to Allison. God had given them each gifts, and a gentleman would appreciate those gifts or not as the mood took him. Others of the debutantes failed to attract her because they did not share a single one of her interests. Some couldn't ride; others were abysmal dancers, and still others preferred to spend each day gossiping incessantly. While she enjoyed a good coz as well as the next person, she found frequent visiting a bit of a bore. In fact, she had found her sister debutantes as a rule lackluster and cowed, depending on their mothers or a gentleman for conversation. Most would never even have considered owning a pet ferret as she did. She had made friends with the few who seemed to have some sense as well as a flair for living. And each one of those, from the sophisticated Lady Janice Willstencraft to sweet Grace Dunsworthy, had been invited to her own ball.

And certainly, it wasn't her financial state that made her view the coming affair with considerably less enthusiasm. Eighteen months ago when her father had died suddenly, leaving them penniless, she had thought she might never have her day. But last January, Genevieve had become engaged to Alan Pentercast, a handsome landowner of considerable fortune. When she had married him in February, he had readily agreed to pay all expenses for Allison's Season. So, here she was, in a luxurious London town house rented through the summer, an entire new stylish wardrobe, and her own lady's maid. That part of her dream had worked out better than she could ever have hoped.

And it wasn't that she feared she'd be compared to her elder sister. Genevieve had been the toast of the *ton* with her hair of spun gold, soft blue eyes, and womanly curves compacted in a tiny frame. Allison was confident that her own flaxen ringlets, vibrant blue eyes, classic features so much like her mother's, and taller, more slender form would still attract enough notice to be called a success. Besides, Genevieve could hardly be called the toast of the *ton* of late. Since their first day in the Mayfair town house, her sister had been pale and listless, prone to tears and unexplainable bouts of illness, particularly right after breakfast. The widow Munroe had threatened to call in a famous London physician, but Genevieve had refused. She claimed she was merely homesick and sent a note home to Wenwood begging Alan to join her in London. Accordingly, the squire was expected at any time, and Allison would be certain to have his handsome presence at her ball.

And it certainly wasn't the ball itself that worried her. She hadn't had much to do with the planning at all. The widow Munroe had been unstinting in her efforts to ensure that every detail was painstakingly perfect. From the selection of music the string quartet was to play to the tiny yellow roses that were to decorate the refreshment tables at the midnight supper, her mother had overlooked nothing. The one hundred guests had been carefully chosen to include the doyens of Society whose approval Allison must meet. It was a tribute to her family's connections as well as her mother's reputation as a hostess that not one person had refused the invitation. Like her mother, she should be in alt.

But the very idea of her come out was making her miserable, and it was entirely Geoffrey Pentercast's fault.

"I do not know why I can't get him out of my mind," she had complained to Genevieve only the day before.

Genevieve had smiled wanly from her seat across the damask-draped breakfast table. "Did you dream of him again last night, love?"

"Yes," Allison had admitted with disgust. "And I find myself thinking of him at the most inappropriate times! Yesterday when I was having the final fittings of my gown, I caught myself wondering whether Geoffrey would like the way it calls attention to my bosom."

Genevieve had choked on her tea. "Allison! I certainly hope you didn't tell Mother!"

Of course she hadn't. She wasn't cork-brained. Her calm, proper mother would have ruined her reputation for restraint if she'd known how often Geoffrey Pentercast intruded on her daughter's mind. Her mother considered Geoffrey's powerful frame and brash manner to be signs of boorishness. Allison found the latter open and honest, and what she thought about the former would have made her mother give up all hope of her daughter's maidenly virtue. Truthfully, she had found him rather annoying growing up together in Wenwood. But when she had returned last Christmas after a six-year absence, she had been surprised to find she rather liked the way his dark-brown eyes twinkled with laughter. She could not imagine what her mother saw that was unlikable. His nose was long and straight, his mouth generous and nearly always set in a wicked grin, and his chin was as firm and confident as his manner. He was broad shouldered and sturdily built, a solid gentleman very unlike some of the spindly shanked dandies she had met in London. And unlike some of the cool, sophisticated London gentlemen, he rode and danced with enthusiasm. All in all, Geoffrey Pentercast was a fine specimen of a man. That was entirely the problem.

She had met any number of gentlemen since her arrival in London. Some were handsome; some were charming; some were intelligent, and a few were all three. Several had made it clear that as soon as she was officially out they would be calling in earnest. One, the Marquis DeGuis, hadn't even waited that long. She had been driving with him twice, riding once, and she had entertained him for visits on four separate occasions. And at Grace Dunsworthy's debut, he had asked her to dance three times. She could scarcely believe it.

Her mother was obviously cautious about his interest. He had survived to the age of thirty immune to the lures of the ladies of London. It did seem too good to be true that such a paragon would seek out Allison.

And he was a paragon. That she could not argue. He was reportedly worth thirty thousand per annum. His jet-black hair, piercing blue eyes, and noble chin made the ladies sigh with delight. His ability with horses, both riding and racing, made the gentlemen sigh with envy. While he was more slender than Geoffrey's muscled bulk, he was a head taller than she was, making her feel deliciously feminine. In fact, he was in every way the sort of gentleman she had always dreamed of attaching.

Only he simply wasn't Geoffrey Pentercast.

For the fourth time in as many days she scolded herself for what was surely misplaced loyalty. She could not be in love with Geoffrey. She would not let herself be. She had known him since attending the vicarage school in the nearby village of Wenwood. Last Christmas, she had thought it entertaining to enter into a mild flirtation with him, which he seemed to enjoy equally as much. In fact, since her sister's marriage to his brother, they had become the best of friends. The problem was, not a single gentleman she had met in London so far, with the possible exception of the ever-so-wonderful Marquis DeGuis, was half so enjoyable to tease nor half so delightful to ride or dance with as Geoffrey Pentercast.

She poked the needle into the white lawn nightcap she was embroidering for her trousseau and glanced across the sitting room fire to where her sister dozed. There was a self-satisfied smile on Genevieve's face that surely had nothing to do with the half-finished pillow cover on her lap. Not for the first time Allison wished for the composure her mother and sister seemed to call on so easily. Genevieve was nothing if not sophisticated and courtly. She moved with confidence and elegance. She was the perfect lady of the manor to Alan's country squire. Allison sometimes felt her own movements seemed precipitous and overly dramatic next to her sister's. True, Genevieve liked to call her wonderfully animated; but watching her sister, Allison wondered whether the *ton* would find her abilities as enviable.

Certainly the Marquis DeGuis was tolerant of her foibles, although she had to admit she did her best to hide them from him. The other day in the park, for example, he had magnanimously insisted that they ride on the Ladies Mile when she knew she was perfectly capable of taking Rotten Row beside him with the rest of the gentlemen riders. Why, she and Geoffrey Pentercast had taken more difficult stretches back home in Wenwood, and at a much faster clip than the marquis was want to try with her! Unfortunately, the fact that she was a bruising rider would have been rather scandalous in London, or so it seemed to her. That was the problem with so many of the people she had met in London—she felt to be accepted by them, she had to be less than what she was. Or perhaps considerably more than what she was capable of being. It was a perplexing problem. No doubt the reason Geoffrey Pentercast was so much on her mind was that, with him, she did not have to be anyone but Allison Ermintrude Munroe.

She shook her head and pulled the needle back out of the cap, giving it an extra tug as she realized she had inadvertently snagged her new pink sarcenet gown. She really had to take herself in hand. She hadn't come to London to pine away for a boy she had known all her life. She had much more important matters to attend to. Her come out would signal to the world that she was a woman grown. And successfully navigating the Season would show her family that she was every bit the lady. Even if her ball would be dull beyond words without someone of Geoffrey's caliber to tease her into a grin, it was still a major accomplishment to be savored. Besides, relying on Geoffrey to make her happy made her just as bad as those debutantes who could not speak without the permission of their mothers. She was better than that.

The butler her mother had hired for the Season moved into the room so silently she almost didn't notice him among the floral pattern that decorated nearly every surface. Although his ramrod-straight posture, impressive build, and no-nonsense manner had endeared him to her mother, Allison found his demeanor cold and forbidding. Coupled with a long nose, determined chin, and thinning gray hair, his gray eyes were all the more judgmental and not a little calculating. Besides, it seemed that, like her mother, he believed young ladies who were not yet formally out should be seldom seen and never heard. Now he cleared his throat to make them aware of his presence.

"What is it, Perkins?" she asked as Genevieve stirred and opened her eyes.

As usual, he ignored her, focusing on her sister. "Pardon my interruption, Mrs. Pentercast, but there are two gentlemen callers here to see you."

Allison tossed her needlework aside in annoyance at his manner even as Genevieve frowned.

"At this hour?" her sister murmured, stifling a yawn. "Please tell them we are no longer receiving."

Perkins bowed and started toward the door.

Allison knew she should abide by her sister's decision, but for once the staid and proper response was completely unsatisfactory. "Wait!" she commanded and had the pleasure of seeing the butler hesitate, most likely weighing the consequences of disobeying so direct an order. "Shouldn't we at least find out who they are, Gen?"

Genevieve nodded. "Of course. How silly of me! I seem to have my head in the clouds recently." The same self-satisfied smile crossed her lips again as she patted down the skirts of her blue kerseymere gown, and Allison frowned at her before returning her gaze to the waiting servant.

"Well, Perkins?" she encouraged him.

Perkins sniffed distastefully, and she wasn't sure whether it was her forward behavior or their guests' he found lacking. "No one of importance, madame. They claim to be relations, but they are not at all dressed like gentlemen. They appear to be dressed for some kind of farming activity."

"Alan!" Genevieve exclaimed, rising.

Allison jumped to her feet. "Now see what you've done, Perkins! You've kept the squire standing about in the cold, and he's the one who pays your salary!"

Perkins paled, but his tread toward the door was stately and composed. "You must be mistaken, miss. However, I will endeavor to inquire again."

"Never mind," Genevieve proclaimed, bustling past him. Allison hurried to follow her. "I intend to see these gentlemen myself. Please go find my mother."

Perkins bowed again. "As you wish, madame."

"I'll wager you my pink beads against your white silk parasol," Allison hissed to her sister as they hurried down the darkly paneled hall toward the entry, "that he won't make the servants' stairs before we reach the front door."

"Foolish bet," Gen hissed back. "I like that parasol too well to risk it on Perkins' ability to move with any speed. And I will never understand his obsession with taking the servants' stair when he could take the main."

The long hall opened onto a two-story entry with a black-and-white marble-tiled floor and white Corinthian columns flanking the solid front door. Backs against the columns stood the underfootman and footman her mother had hired for the Season. While their arms were at the sides of their navy livery, their gazes rested with suspicion on the two characters who waited. One stood square in the center of the entryway in a pool of yellow light from the brass chandelier overhead, worn greatcoat flapping about his muddy country boots—Alan Pentercast, just as his wife had guessed.

And behind him, half in shadow, grinning at Allison in the most audacious manner that somehow made her heart stop, stood his brother Geoffrey.

Two

Geoffrey Pentercast had the satisfaction of watching the ever-animated Allison Munroe take one look at him and freeze. Her sister was not so restrained, leaping into his brother's arms. Behind him, he could feel the silent hostility of the footmen melt away as they realized they were indeed dealing with family and not some ruffians intent on ransacking the family estate. He ignored them as well as the rampant display of affection in front of him and gazed at Allison around his brother's bent head.

She knew she was staring at him in the most abstracted manner, but she couldn't seem to help herself. Geoffrey told himself he ought to find her regard flattering, but it actually made him feel rather self-conscious. Had he changed so much since she had last seen him? His hand went of its own volition to touch the beaver top hat the butler had refused to take, feeling the dark-brown hair curling around the brim. Or was it that his greatcoat, and the brown tweed jacket and trousers beneath, were as coated as the hat with dust from riding the better part of two days to get here? Either way, he wasn't sure what her careful study might mean.

She certainly hadn't changed. The flaxen ringlets were just as soft around her narrow face; her eyes, bluer than the bluest sky, were just as bright. He didn't remember seeing that pink dress she wore before, but then he thought Alan had mentioned she had been given an entire new wardrobe. With a pang, he wondered whether more had changed than her clothes when she had arrived in London. He wanted more than anything else to ask, but she was still staring at him in that odd way. In self-defense, he did the only thing he could think of. He winked at her.

Allison blushed, flustered. Why did he have to show up now, just when she had been on the point of taking herself in hand? Determined, she turned her attention to her sister and brother-in-law, noting for the first time their rather jubilant reunion.

"I wouldn't twirl her about like that if I were you," she told Alan, who was indeed spinning his wife about in a most giddy fashion. "She hasn't been all that well."

Geoffrey frowned with concern, and Alan halted abruptly, holding his wife at arms' length, brown eyes so like his brother's gazing at her warily. "What's this? You never mentioned you were unwell in the note."

"I had more important matters to impart," Genevieve scolded, laughing.

Allison had to admit the spinning did not seem to have troubled her sister. Indeed, Gen positively glowed. Of course, it could have been her husband's presence. Alan was in some ways even more handsome than Geoffrey, with his superior height that was every bit as tall as the marquis. He was also more polished than his brother, although he often chose to wear the rough clothes of the country squire rather than the tailored lines of a Corinthian. He also carried with him an air of authority that sat well on his broad shoulders. Still, given a choice, Allison much preferred Geoffrey's honest, unaffected manner and powerful frame.

"But you said you sent for him because you were homesick," Allison protested, not sure whether to be amused or annoyed. "If you didn't tell him you were ill, just what did you tell him to get him to come all this distance so quickly?"

Geoffrey grinned at her. "They've been married less than three months, moonling. What do you *think* she told him?"

Allison felt her blush deepen, and she refused to meet his eye. Obviously she had conveniently forgotten his most annoying trait—his ability to catch her off guard.

"I assure you that I would come quickly whenever Genevieve called for me, Miss Allison," Alan replied, eyes never leaving his wife's radiant face. "But this time she told me something that could not have kept me away."

Allison glanced between their besotted faces. "Well, what was it?"

Genevieve broke her husband's gaze with obvious difficulty. "There's a reason I've been ill, dearest, but I thought Alan should know first. We're going to have a baby."

"Oh, Gen!" Allison cried, throwing her arms about them both. "How marvelous!"

"Congratulations, old man!" Geoffrey agreed wholeheartedly, pummeling his brother affectionately on the back. "And you too, sister Genevieve."

"Thank you both." Genevieve laughed even as Alan attempted to fend them off.

"Oh," Allison clarioned, "but you must tell Mother!" She glanced back at the empty staircase rising behind them. "Of course, it would be a lot easier if Perkins would move faster than an elderly turtle."

"Curious fellow," Alan agreed with typical good nature. "I believe he thought we were lying when we said we were related."

"I'll wager you miss Chimes," Geoffrey added, thinking of the elderly unorthodox butler and man-of-all-work who had been their servant in Wenwood. "He may not be as proper as your mother would want, but he has always taken good care of you all at the Abbey."

"I doubt he'd care to come to London now," Allison replied with a sigh. "He didn't much appreciate being left behind, and Chimes is awfully good about keeping a grudge."

"He'll eventually forgive us," Gen predicted. "He knew he wouldn't have much fun here. And Mother was adamant that we needed a more polished staff if we were to send Allison up properly."

Geoffrey snorted. "As if she needs the right kind of servants to be noticed. I'll wager you've already had more than your share of callers."

He regretted it as soon as he'd said it. The thought had been too much on his mind all the way up to London; he didn't much want to hear it confirmed.

Allison preened, and his heart sank. "There have been a few gentlemen, two or three a day some days."

"Most notably the Marquis DeGuis," Genevieve confirmed before Geoffrey could comment. "If you think Allison is insufferable about it, you should see Mother."

"And she will be even more insufferable when you tell her your news," Allison added, all purpose now that the initial meeting was over. "So, let us get you settled." She ignored Geoffrey's scowl and motioned the footmen to take their guests' hats and coats and to take the two valises near the door to waiting guest chambers. As soon as that had been achieved, she pushed her sister and brother-in-law toward the stairs.

Genevieve linked her arm in Alan's, and they obligingly went ahead up the wide polished stair that curved up to the second floor. Allison made to follow, but Geoffrey caught her arm, holding her back as the footmen hurried off toward the servants' stairs at the back of the house.

"Let them go. I'd like a word with you."

Allison tossed her head, ready to refuse anyone who spoke to her in so proprietary a manner. But she gazed into his face and saw only concern. By the way her haughty look evaporated, Geoffrey realized he was obviously showing more than he intended and struggled to regain control of himself.

"Is something wrong?" she asked, glancing toward her sister's retreating back to make sure they were out of hearing. "Is Alan not happy about this baby?"

"Alan is in transports, as you can see," he assured her. "As if all those presents he showered on your sister, one for each of the twelve days of Christmas, weren't enough, I imagine he'll buy half the toys in London for the tyke. It was all I could do to get him to rest the horses on the way up, and now I know why. No, Alan is beyond delighted." He swallowed and plunged ahead. "I wish to speak about you."

Allison paled, glancing again at her sister and his brother, who suddenly seemed too far away. "But I want to see Mother's face when she hears the news," she protested, not at all sure she was ready to hear what he had to say. She started up the stairs again, and Geoffrey had no choice but to fall into step beside her.

"Your mother wouldn't get excited if we told her the Monarchy had collapsed," he tried pointing out. "I daresay news of her first grandchild will barely raise an eyebrow." He touched her arm again, slowing her. "Please, Allison. We won't get much chance for a private word, if I know your family. And that's the only reason I came along on this mad ride."

She sighed and stopped at the top of the stair, knowing he was right. She made sure Gen and Alan were headed down the darkly paneled corridor toward the upstairs sitting room and turned to him with trepidation. "Very well, Geoffrey. What is it that is so important that it brings you all the way to London?"

"Concern for you," he replied, and despite all his efforts, his deep voice came out entirely too much like a caress. "I've missed you, Allison."

Allison felt as if a candle had been lit inside her, spreading warmth and light around her heart. She almost blurted out her own feelings of late, then realized she was supposed to be acting like a lady. "I find myself thinking of you often as well," she replied with maidenly restraint.

"You do?" It was exactly what he had been hoping for. He seized her hand and pressed it between his own. Her slender fingers were lost in the massive grip. "You can't know how happy I am to hear you say that. I just want you to know, Allison, that you needn't go through all this."

He didn't want her to have a Season? The thought was so foreign, even for all her recent apprehensions, that Allison pulled her hand back, frowning. "What do you mean? Are you talking about my Season or do you speak of the ball? Of course I must go through with that. The invitations have already been sent."

"Not the ball, moonling," he smiled, the old pet name for her too easy on his tongue. "Of course you'll want to do that. I know your fondness for dancing. I'm speaking of your London Season. You don't need it."

Allison shook her head, frown deepening. "Yes, I must have my Season. Every young lady of proper family is expected to have one. Sometimes I feel as if I've been waiting my entire life for it."

"But, Allison," he protested, determined to make her see, "the purpose of a London Season is to find a suitable match. You have no reason to do that."

She could not be understanding him. The only reason not to look for a husband was if she had one already.

Geoffrey Pentercast, even at twenty-two, was entirely too young to want to settle down and marry now. She knew she must be staring at him, her shock showing in every line of her body, because he hurried on before she could protest.

"I know I'm not much of a candidate in your mother's eyes. She'll most likely prefer this marquis fellow."

He was proposing. She couldn't seem to breathe. She couldn't seem to move. She couldn't even seem to think beyond the fact that he was proposing to her.

When she still did not speak, dread seized Geoffrey. He grabbed her shoulders and stared down into her eyes, furious and frightened at the same time. "And perhaps you prefer the marquis as well. Damnation! I knew I shouldn't have let you go like that. Do you love him? Has he offered? Am I too late?"

She shook him off, but she was sure he must have felt her trembling. She fought to regain control of her thoughts. She must refuse him, of course she must refuse him. She wasn't in love with anyone, not Geoffrey and not the marquis.

"No, Geoffrey," she said firmly, "to all three questions. And no, I will not give up my Season, not even for you."

"But," he started, and she laid her finger to close his lips. The warmth against her skin almost started her trembling anew.

"No, Geoffrey," she repeated. "I know most girls go through all this to catch a husband, but that's not why it's important to me. This Season is the only way I'll ever have standing in my family."

He frowned, reaching to remove her finger from his lips. "What do you mean, *standing*?"

Allison sighed, finding it hard to explain something

she had never told another soul. "Have you never noticed how everyone treats me, Mother most of all?"

"No. What has that to do with a London Season?"

"Everything," she told him. Then she straightened her shoulders, determined to make her point. "To Mother, to Genevieve, even to Alan, and especially to that detestable butler, I'm still a child. They feel perfectly justified in ignoring what I want and what I say, out of some parental kind of logic that only their thoughts and feelings have value. This Season is my chance to show them I'm an adult, Geoffrey. I saw how Mother's reaction to Gen changed once she'd come out. Suddenly, Mother could consult Gen on household management and bunion remedies, as if a series of balls and dinners had somehow endowed my sister with all feminine knowledge. If I marry you, if I marry anyone, before I've achieved that status, I will never have any standing in this family. Can you understand that?"

He took a deep breath, relieved she had not fallen in love with anyone else, but saddened by her refusal to give up her Season all the same. "I think so. I feel the same way myself sometimes, especially around Alan. He and my mother both watch me as if they expect me to belch at the dinner table or wear muddy boots to bed."

Allison giggled. "I daresay you've done both."

His grin reappeared. "I daresay you're right. But since neither is a crime punishable by death, I fail to see why anyone cares." He sobered, reaching out to touch her cheek and sending a wave of warmth through her as he did so. "I'm not perfect Allison. And I cannot bear the thought that some perfect gentleman may steal you away from me. Is there nothing I can do to dissuade you from this course?"

If he only knew how close he was to doing just that. His gaze warmed, and she was afraid she had given herself away. He moved toward her, closing the short distance between their lips. She could see the desire plain in his deep brown eyes. If he kissed her now she would lose everything. Before he could make good the threat of his gentle smile, she whirled away from him and lifted her skirts to clatter up the stairs.

"Nothing," she called back over her shoulder. "So you may as well give up now."

Three

Allison was completely out of breath by the time she located her mother in the upstairs sitting room. As she had suspected, Perkins had reached her to inform her she had guests only moments before Gen and Alan had walked into the room. Allison knew her breathlessness had nothing to do with her mother's calm response to the news that she would soon be a grandmother. As Geoffrey had predicted, the widow Munroe offered the slightest of smiles to Alan and a correctly placed kiss on the cheek to Genevieve. Allison was sure her own cheeks must be flaming red and hurried to a chair in a dimly lit corner where no one would notice her.

Geoffrey followed her in. He noticed how she scampered away from him. Much as he would have liked to continue the conversation on the stair, now did not seem like a time to badger Allison. Besides, she had given him much to think about. He caught the widow Munroe eyeing him with distaste and tactfully withdrew to the fireplace, picking up the wrought-iron poker and stirring the coals for an excuse to do something. He was sure if anyone else noticed him, they'd think he was being surly, but he didn't much care and no one noticed. His brother and sister-in-law were too preoccupied with plans for the future to notice either him or Allison.

Allison, for one, was thankful for being ignored. She

studied Geoffrey's profile from under lowered lashes. The determined set of his generous mouth more than anything showed his annoyance that she had refused his suit. If one could call his veiled proposal a suit. Now that she thought about it, he had been rather circumspect, especially for Geoffrey Pentercast. For all her admiration of his form and enjoyment of his company, she had never thought he was in love with her. The way he still delighted in teasing her made him seem like an older brother.

And was he as jealous of her beaux as he seemed? She had certainly teased him about that a number of times in the past, bragging about how many men she would keep dangling when she reached London. She supposed she had implied that they would be better men than he was. It was little wonder he saw her impending come out as a threat to their friendship. Surely that was what had driven him to go so far as to suggest he might offer for her should she give it up. She couldn't let that supposed offer deter her. She liked Geoffrey about as much as it was possible to like anyone, but he truly didn't fit the picture of the man she had always assumed she'd marry.

He obviously didn't fit her mother's picture of what the next week would be like either. The widow Munroe accepted Alan's offer to act as escort to balls and dinners with a regal inclination of her head. However, when she realized that that escort included the company of his brother, she went so far as to actually frown.

"I do not believe young Mr. Pentercast will find London at all amusing," she told Alan. "He would be far happier returning to Somerset to wait for you."

A shower of sparks shot up the chimney and the coals glowed from Geoffrey's sudden vicious prodding.

Ignoring him, Alan smiled at his mother-in-law indulgently. "That may be true, but I don't like the thought

of him on the road alone. Besides, a bit of town bronze
will do him good. However, if you prefer, Geoffrey,
Genevieve, and I could repair to a hotel for our visit."

Allison watched, holding her breath, while her mother
visibly weighed the difficulties of having her oldest
daughter living elsewhere in a delicate condition with
having Geoffrey Pentercast underfoot. Genevieve's presence thankfully won. "That should not be necessary,
squire. I'm sure we can find something useful for your
brother to do while he is with us."

"How very gracious," Geoffrey muttered. "I'm sure
there are large pieces of furniture that need moving or
perhaps the stables need cleaning."

Allison bit back a laugh as her mother's nostrils
flared. Still, her reply was calm.

"Nothing so onerous, Mr. Pentercast. I merely thought
you might accompany Allison and her set on their many
calls. Another gentleman is always welcome among the
young ladies, I believe."

"If it means watching other fellows make cow eyes at
Allison," he growled, scowling at Allison so furiously
that she wanted nothing more than to box his ears,
"count me out." He straightened away from the fire,
suddenly tired of the whole affair. "I might as well go
home, Alan. There's nothing for me here."

Allison shook her head. So much for undying devotion. She'd forgotten how much he resembled a spoiled
child when crossed. She stood up and shook out her
skirts. "You may stay or you may go, Mr. Pentercast. It
makes little difference to me. Besides, the young ladies
of my circle would not know what to do with you. *They*
are used to dealing with gentlemen."

Geoffrey bridled, but Alan stepped warningly to his
side. "Now, Miss Allison, you know Geoffrey can be
quite charming when he puts his mind to it." He
squeezed his brother's shoulder. "Can't you, Geoffrey?"

Geoffrey's brown eyes glittered dangerously. "Tremendously charming. Perhaps I ought to stay the whole Season, just to prove it."

"That will hardly be necessary," her mother interjected entirely too quickly. "However, I'm sure your company the next week should be . . . interesting."

He bowed to her, but his eyes strayed to Allison, who had to stop herself from cringing at the frustration there. "Interesting it shall be, madame. I promise."

Allison began the next day prepared to do battle. This was her Season; she had planned for it, worked for it, waited for it. She was not about to let one of Geoffrey Pentercast's moods spoil even so much as a day of it.

Consequently, she got up at her usual early hour, fed Pippin her ferret and tousled his fur, then met her cousin Margaret Munroe for their daily constitutional around Mayfair.

Allison knew her mother did not appreciate Margaret. Few people did. Margaret Munroe, a second cousin to Allison and Genevieve, could only be called an Original. Her coal-black hair was starting to gray at the tender age of twenty, making it look as if she had sprinkled her braided bun with salt. Her sharp, crystal-blue eyes looked out at an imposing height that even Allison could not match. Yet if anything could be termed the least bit disproportional about her, it was her bustline, whose generous proportions often had the gentlemen raising their quizzing glasses as she passed. As if she didn't make a striking enough figure, she had an opinion about every subject, and she wasn't afraid to state those opinions, loudly and at great length. This tendency, coupled with an innate curiosity she found impossible to curb, made her the bane of most social gatherings. Like Allison, however, she had two qualities that endeared her to at least some members of the *ton:* there wasn't a horse she couldn't ride and there wasn't a partner she couldn't outlast on the dance floor. Allison found her company invigorating and her conversation stimulating.

That morning was no exception. Allison was not long in commenting on Geoffrey's arrival the night before. Of course, Margaret had thoughts on the matter.

"That's the one you were prosing on about the last few weeks," she interrupted Allison in midexplanation as they strode along the Mayfair street. "The burly fellow from Somerset?"

"Yes," Allison sighed. "I truly didn't expect him here—and attempting to propose of all things."

"Certainly not," Margaret nodded, but she winked conspiratorially. "Although it sounds as if it might be enjoyable to have him about with us the next week or so."

"You'll have fun. He'll give as good as you give," Allison promised, grinning at the thought of Margaret and Geoffrey in a horse race. Then she sobered, knowing that it would do neither's reputation any good. "Although Mother won't like it above half. And I don't want to think what will happen should he meet the marquis."

Margaret clasped her hands behind her back and increased her strides. "You are intent on capturing him, then?"

"The marquis?" Allison gasped, faltering in her attempt to keep up. "I would never be so bold! He's the most sough-after gentleman on the marriage mart, the catch of the Season! What makes you think I could possibly set my cap for him?"

Margaret shook her head, slowing to allow Allison to reach her. "Every other young lady has set her cap for him. What makes you immune?" She grinned again and nudged Allison in the ribs. "Or is it Geoffrey Pentercast you favor?"

Allison felt herself blushing. "At the moment, I truly cannot tell you." She eyed her cousin's regal profile as they continued their walk. "Margaret, have you ever been in love?"

Margaret seemed to trip on something in the way, stumbling to a halt. Her face, when she turned to her friend, was redder than Allison's. "Why . . . why do you ask?" she managed.

"You have, haven't you?" Allison asked suspiciously. Then she grinned, reaching out to squeeze Margaret's arm. "It's all right, you silly goose! You can tell me."

"No, I can't," Margaret said firmly, taking off once more at a fierce trot. "It's entirely too personal, if you please."

"Well, I like that!" Allison declared. "The woman who asked Lord Baminger which of his opera dances he preferred, refusing to speak on her own love affairs? You cannot get away with it, you know."

"I shall get away with it," Margaret maintained. "I refuse to reveal his name, so you may as well stop asking."

Allison regarded the determined set of her jaw and the way her hands were balled in fists at her sides. "Very well," she conceded. "I won't press you. However, I must ask. What is it like?"

Margaret smiled knowingly. "It is delightful above anything, and painful too. A sort of warm feeling in your chest that never leaves you, and only glows brighter when you think of him or chance upon him."

Allison sighed with longing. "How lovely. Will you be announcing your engagement soon?"

"Doubtful," Margaret replied cheerfully. "He doesn't even know I exist."

"Margaret!" Allison cried, dismayed.

Her friend only grinned at her and refused to say another word on the matter for the rest of their walk.

Allison was still considering her cousin's confession, and description of love, when she returned to change into her royal-blue riding habit for a scheduled ride through Hyde Park with Lady Janice Willstencraft. Unfortunately, before she could make any decisions, Geoffrey caught up with her in the entryway.

Geoffrey had slept in late, rising for breakfast just in time to see Allison heading for her room. A whispered conversation with a servant was all it took to learn she was changing to go riding. He ordered toast, shaved while he waited, and crammed the bread in his mouth while he pulled on his own green wool riding outfit. He was downstairs lounging in the entryway when she attempted to leave with her friend. It was only a matter of smiling politely to get an invitation from the stunning Lady Janice to accompany them.

She wasn't the kind of person he would have thought Allison would like. Her exterior was lovely and cool, especially in that wine-colored riding habit, but the looks she gave him out of the corners of those green eyes could only be called smoldering. Her obvious attempts to flirt only made him uncomfortable. He found himself watching Allison to see if she had picked up the same tricks, but was pleased to see Allison seemed more interested in the lines of the horses they passed than the gentlemen who rode them.

For Allison's part, she was surprised and a little suspicious that Geoffrey seemed so well behaved. When they had agreed to let him accompany them, he had bowed and kissed Lady Janice's hand, of all things! He had then given each of them an arm to escort them to the waiting horses. Now he made witty conversation that set the usually refined Lady Janice to giggling until Allison had to grit her teeth at the sound. However, when he found they intended to ride the Ladies Mile, he quickly left them to their own devices. Allison could only sigh in envy as he pelted off for more challenging areas of the park where usually only the men rode.

Lady Janice obviously mistook the source of her sigh. "What a rather fascinating study in manliness," she remarked.

"I beg your pardon?" Allison gasped.

Lady Janice smiled, looking worldly wise for all her eighteen years. "Come now, Allison, you must admit that Mr. Pentercast is so much more interesting than many of the other fellows we've met in London."

"Well, I once thought so," Allison allowed. "But I didn't think many other people would share my feelings."

"Most likely not." Janice nodded sagely, shiny black ringlets bouncing under her fetching wine velvet riding hat. "Mr. Pentercast seems to be an Original, not unlike yourself, Allison. It takes a person of rare intellect and vision to appreciate an Original."

Allison snorted, thinking of Margaret, pining away while her love was unaware. "Rare intellect or little intellect. Do you honestly think my mother would prefer him to any of my other beaux?"

Lady Janice giggled again. "Oh, most certainly not. For all Mr. Pentercast's many qualities, he still cannot hold a candle to the Marquis DeGuis."

Allison laughed as she guided Blackie around a copse of trees. "Certainly not. I cannot imagine two more different men."

"Mr. Pentercast has no title; he isn't wealthy, and he is only a second son," Janice continued, counting the reasons with a wave of her riding quirt. "Although I would say that each is sufficiently handsome, in his own way."

"Oh, I'll grant you that the marquis is a paragon,"

Allison agreed. Yet, for some reason, she felt compelled to defend Geoffrey. "But do you never feel he is perhaps a bit *too* perfect?"

Lady Janice trained emerald eyes on her. "My dear Allison, how can anyone be *too* perfect?"

Allison shrugged, scowling. "Oh, I don't know. I only know that there are a few things about him which trouble me."

"Such as?" Janice frowned.

"First," Allison replied, "he seems to have a difficult time speaking beyond the most commonplace. He will prose on about the weather or who was at the latest ball we attended, but nothing of any depth. I never thought I'd say this, Lady Janice, but I think we might get along better together if we ever found something to passionately agree, or even disagree, about."

"Certainly you would not want to disagree," Janice protested.

"Whyever not? It seems to me that a woman should be able to have her opinions, regardless of whether they happen to agree with her husband's."

"Certainly she might have them," Janice agreed, "although she would most likely not state them in public."

Allison wrinkled her nose. "Stuff and nonsense. I could never marry so tyrannical a husband."

"Then you are fortunate to have so many suitors from which to choose," Janice replied. "And for all your complaints of him, I must say that the marquis seems quite smitten with you."

"Do you truly think so?" Allison asked, a tremor of excitement rising at the thought. After only a second's consideration, however, she dismissed the notion. "Wouldn't you think that if he were truly smitten," she told her friend, "he would attempt some form of familiarity?"

Janice frowned at her. "What do you mean?"

"Oh, I don't know. Shouldn't he want to speak to me of things no one else should hear? Shouldn't he want to be alone with me? Maybe even steal a kiss?"

Again Allison felt herself studied. "Dear Allison, do you mean to tell me you have never found a way to get the marquis alone? Oh my dear, you truly must! I would never accept an offer from any gentleman unless we had kissed. How would one determine the level of compatibility otherwise?"

Allison stared at her, riding so calmly beside her. "But I'd heard you'd already collected six offers. Does that mean . . ."

Lady Janice smiled again, green eyes cryptic. "You may infer what you like. I will only marry a man whose kiss sets me ablaze."

"That seems unaccountably high expectations for a kiss," Allison maintained.

Lady Janice shrugged. "That is my choice. And I suggest if you wish to know whether you like the Marquis DeGuis or Mr. Pentercast better, you let each steal a kiss."

Allison thought of the kiss Geoffrey had stolen last Christmas. At the time, it had surprised and alarmed her, but she felt she had matured since then. Would she react differently now? Just thinking he might have kissed her the evening he had arrived had made her tremble all over. And how would she react to the marquis's kiss? That was almost too overwhelming to think about. It almost made Margaret's unspoken love seem palatable.

She had to admit, however, that Janice was quite right that, on the marriage mart, the Marquis DeGuis was a much greater prize than Geoffrey Pentercast. However, she reminded herself, she was not going through this Season to catch a husband. Still, it was difficult to dismiss so dashing a suitor as the marquis. Twice during

the week before her ball he called to take her driving
through the park. As the second time was only a day
after her conversations with Margaret and Lady Janice,
she was sure her behavior could only be called contrary.
But if he noticed, he gave no indication.

"The weather is quite summer-like today," he mused
as they tooled toward Hyde Park in his white-enameled
gig.

Allison glanced up at the cloudless blue sky, barely
tainted with smoke from the Londoners' fires on so
warm a day for April. "Yes, it's lovely. Do you think it
will continue warm like this?"

"Perhaps," he replied thoughtfully. "But the weather
is ever unpredictable. I daresay the fellow who learns to
decipher it will be famous."

Allison brightened at the hint of a deeper subject.
"How would one do that, do you suppose?"

He smiled indulgently. "I couldn't begin to say, Miss
Munroe. I'm sure wiser heads than ours will one day
solve the problem. Did you say you had seen Her Grace
the duchess last week at the Baminger ball?"

"Yes," Allison sighed, relegated once more to banality.
"She requested that I give you her regards."

"How very kind." He nodded.

Allison watched him from the corner of her eye. He
kept his gaze on the road ahead, calm, unruffled, care-
free. She studied the line of his jaw, the hint of softness
in his lips. Janice's suggestion came to mind and she
forced it away. She could hardly let him kiss her on a
crowded Mayfair street. Besides, he didn't look real as
he sat beside her in his bottle-green coat and tan chamois breeches. That cravat was entirely too white and too
intricately folded. It made her own sky-blue pelisse seem
rumpled and worn. She had an overwhelming desire to
reach up, knock off his top hat, and muss up his hair.

She sighed. She had been excited beyond anything

that this impeccable gentleman might consider courting her. Why was it she found his perfection so frustrating all of a sudden? If she couldn't rearrange his attire, the least she could do was to say something irritating just to see how he would react. Perhaps it was the imp in her that made her do just that. "By the way, the duchess was wearing the most horrible gown I've ever seen. I do not know what possessed her to don it!"

She was rewarded with the slightest of frowns, and suddenly she was reminded of her mother. "Indeed," he replied in a tone that could only be called quelling. "I have always found the duchess to have the very best taste, in clothing as well as other matters."

She wanted to argue with him, but she couldn't very well malign a dear little old lady who had been very kind to her. "Yes, of course," she replied with a sigh, giving up. "No doubt she was given bad advice on that particular outfit and was too kind to refuse it."

The marquis's satisfied smile returned. "No doubt. And how is your family?"

"All well," Allison told him, returning to the conventional conversation. She brightened again, thinking of her sister. "In fact, my sister has announced she is to have a baby."

To her surprise, the frown reappeared. "Indeed. How very inconvenient for you. I imagine she will be returning to Somerset quite soon then."

"Just after my come out," Allison confirmed, wondering why that should trouble him. "She thinks the baby is due in early November, but she wants to be home to set up the nursery and attend to other matters well in advance."

"I'm sure you'll miss her in London," he murmured.

Allison couldn't help feeling touched by his comment. "I'm sure I will. But as I will be joining her as soon as the summer is over, I won't have long to wait."

He glanced over at her, and she had to fight not to frown at the calculating look in his clear blue eyes. "You plan to return to the country in September, then?"

Allison nodded. "Yes, that was always my plan. I understood most of the *ton* repairs to the country for the summer, but Mother wants to stay on as long as possible."

"I see," he replied. "And how is your mother?"

The moment had passed, and she was sure she had missed something. She continued answering his carefully distant questions, but he volunteered nothing more that might help her understand where his concern might be based. She caught herself wishing the dashing marquis was half as forthright as Geoffrey Pentercast. It might not have been easy, but it would have been a great deal more interesting.

Four

Geoffrey Pentercast stood in the hall, just two doors from Allison's bedchamber, and called himself a coward. What kind of man let a pair of sky-blue eyes and a pretty pout deter him from his chosen course of action? When he had hastened to London beside Alan, he had forgotten just how easily Allison could move him to compassion as well as laughter. As he had confessed on his first night, the only reason he had come to London was to propose to Allison. Ever since she had left, he had fretted over whether some fancy London buck would beat him to it.

His mother and brother might have despaired that he would ever be fit for polite society, but Geoffrey was at heart a traditionalist. A man was supposed to have a jolly good time in his youth and then settle down with a nice girl and have children. While Geoffrey was the first to admit he felt a little young at twenty-two to be settling down just yet, he wasn't about to let some other fellow claim what was obviously the perfect mate for Geoffrey.

And Allison was perfect. She was clever, she was pretty, and she had curves in all the right places. But the best thing about Allison was that she wouldn't make him settle all that much. He was sure Allison wouldn't mind if he continued to visit the Wenwood tavern from time to time, although he'd probably have to give up any ideas of bedding Molly Erring who served ale and other things there. And he didn't imagine Allison would protest if he decided they were going to attend every one of the assemblies at Barnsley Grange, although he wouldn't be allowed to dance with Mary Delacourte or any of the other unmarried ladies anymore.

In many ways, Allison was more like one of his friends from the village than what he had thought a wife would be. He could talk to Allison. He never remembered his father and mother talking about anything more intimate than how many eggs the prize goose had laid. He and Allison talked about far more important things, like how they felt about matters. Why, over the twelve days of Christmas alone, they had discussed the reasons their families feuded, the identify of the vandal who had been terrorizing the neighborhood, and their fathers' deaths! They'd spent over an hour at the wedding reception for his brother and her sister pondering what would make a good marriage. At the time, he had thought her insistence on a romantic feeling as the basis for marrying a bit naive, but since then he had realized she had a point. He certainly felt that feeling. And he couldn't imagine discussing such matters with any other girl.

Yes, Allison was perfect. He couldn't take the chance that someone else would notice her many excellent qualities. Like the way she laughed, with all her being, not a simper or a fluffy giggle like other girls. Allison's laughs made her chest jiggle in the most delightful manner. And then there was the way she danced—with hands and feet and frame in motion, not at all like some other girls who tried to mince through a lively country dance as if it were some courtly minuet. When Allison danced, her cheeks turned rosy and her breath came in delighted gasps and she was very likely to bump into a fellow in all the right places. On top of all that, Allison was kindhearted and fun-loving. Surely some other gentleman with more to offer than a second son from the country would notice her.

But he hadn't been able to bring himself to truly propose since their conversation on the stair the first night he had arrived. He hadn't realized that her family treated her with anything less than respect; but after a week in their company, he knew exactly the kind of behavior that had made Allison reach that conclusion. Her mother—and Genevieve, too, for that matter—was constantly harping on her behavior, when anyone could see she was smarter and more animated than any of the sorry specimens of womanhood they trotted out as examples. After the last week, he could safely say that Lady Janice was far too calculating and Grace Dunsworthy was an idiot.

He wasn't entirely sure he believed that a London Season would transform Allison in her family's eyes, but she was obviously certain of it. He would be the greatest villain alive if he tried to deter her. So, instead, he had to watch, helpless, as her mother attempted to launch her into the shark-infested waters of Society, knowing that every ball, every drive, every dinner party took her farther beyond his reach.

Not that he was happily included in any of the events, despite the widow's comments his first night. The widow Munroe made it clear he was something to be tolerated but not encouraged. To do her justice, he hadn't exactly been the best guest at the last ball of hers he had attended. Loosing Allison's pet ferret at the Munroe Epiphany party last January had been done in a fit of childish pique, he had to admit. Even though he had comported himself as much like a gentleman as he was capable of at his brother's wedding and the reception afterward, she still did not think him a suitable escort. Accordingly, she found one reason after another why he could not accompany them on their many outings.

Worse, when he was allowed to join them, she attempted to pair him with one of the young ladies of Allison's circle, most often Grace Dunsworthy.

To Geoffrey, Grace was obviously another testimony to Allison's kind heart. The girl was pretty enough, with light-brown hair that she frequently wore either in ringlets or piled up with wisps about her heart-shaped face. She also possessed a pair of large, pale-blue eyes that always seemed just the slightest bit melancholy. She was too slender for Geoffrey's taste; she looked like a frail ethereal creature when standing next to his bulk. What made her an insupportable companion, besides the fact that paying attention to her kept him from Allison, was her distracted manner. She seemed to have a difficult time following the many conversations that usually went on at any outing with several animated young people, her wide blue eyes swiveling from this one to that in frequent amazement. And she had absolutely no sense of the ridiculous, treating any teasing remark of his as if he had actually meant it. Consequently, when she did attempt to join the conversation, her confusion and innocent response actually served to stop conversation altogether. He had to be careful when he talked to her not to call her Miss Dimwitty.

And then there was that butler. Geoffrey had grown up with Munson, an impressive fellow, running the manor in Wenwood, so he knew the best to which a butler might aspire. He also knew Chimes, the Munroes' butler at the Abbey, who could only be called an imp and certainly one of the least effective butlers around. This Perkins fellow was something else entirely. Geoffrey had never met anyone more calculated to raise his hackles. The man was regimented, overly fastidious, and downright glum. And he seemed to be in league with the widow Munroe to keep Geoffrey away from Allison.

Yes, Geoffrey had barely been able to control himself

all week long. It was hard to be proud of his performance, but he took some satisfaction in the fact that he had kept himself from selfishly proposing to Allison, stopped himself from walking away in disgust from Grace Dunsworthy, and refrained from striking the butler.

And now it was the night of the ball.

He glanced down at the black cutaway coat and white breeches Alan had ordered for him to wear. Even to his eye they looked rumpled; but as he had been unwilling to use Perkins's questionable services as valet, he supposed the clothes would have to do. At least his cravat was an immaculate white, even if it were knotted simply at his throat rather than tied in some complicated fold with a foreign name. And he'd have preferred to wear wool socks and Hessians rather than the white stockings and black pumps. However, much as he would have liked to blame the uncomfortable attire for his hesitation in the hall, he knew it was more than that. Tonight Allison would be formally introduced to Society. It was his last chance to make her see reason before every eligible bachelor of the *ton* crowded him out.

He had been trying half-heartedly all day to get her alone, but between the final fittings of her ball gown and her mother's constant presence, he had failed. There were only two more hours left before the guests began arriving. He had to screw up his courage and demand a moment of her time. But each time he tried, he remembered those sapphire eyes as she'd pleaded with him to try to understand why this blasted Season was so important to her. And then he felt petty and selfish.

He turned on his heel and strode back to his room, slamming the door shut behind him. Was he an idiot to keep torturing himself this way? Allison had made her choice. She had even done him the honor of ex-

plaining her reasons when she owed him no such ex-
planation. This was her moment of glory. He should
leave her to it.

But as he paced about the room, pausing only long
enough to kick the iron fender on the marble fireplace
in frustration (and bruise his toe in the process), doubts
renewed their attack on his resolve. What if she became
the toast of the *ton* as her sister had done? What if some
titled personage found her vivacious manner irresistible?
He hadn't met this DeGuis fellow yet, but all of Allison's
friends, especially Miss Dunsworthy, positively gloated
over the man. What if the fabled marquis came up to
scratch that very night and proposed? Geoffrey couldn't
sit idly by and watch Allison be snatched away.

He stalked back to the door resolutely and marched
down the long hall to Allison's room. He knew he could
hardly invite himself into her bedchamber; he was courting trouble just by standing outside her door. Still, the
matter was urgent. He pulled himself up to his full
height and rapped on the panel.

"Allison," he declared loudly enough to be heard
through the solid door, "I'd like a word with you before
you go downstairs." His voice seemed to echo up and
down the hall, and he glanced guiltily over his shoulder
to make sure no other doors were opening in curiosity.
Then the door in front of him whipped wide and he
whirled to face the woman in the doorway. She was
large, dark-haired, and rather flustered looking. She
wore the black bombazine and white apron and cap of
a lady's maid.

"I'm sorry, sir," she gasped out. "Miss Allison is with
her mother, who wished to supervise her toilette this
evening. I'm sure you'll see her downstairs in a bit."

Geoffrey nodded, turning to go, disappointment like
a stone in his gut. The maid turned from him, muttering as she gazed down at the plate in her hand. Geof-

frey's gaze followed her own, focusing in surprise on the small cubes of what was surely raw meat.

"What are you doing?" He frowned.

The maid jumped, nearly upsetting the plate. "Begging your pardon, sir, but I'm trying to feed Miss Allison's creature. She said she was too distracted to do it herself tonight. Only I haven't a clue how to go about it."

"Allison's creature?" Geoffrey's frown deepened.

The maid nodded nervously. "Yes, sir, if you please, sir. I don't know much about animals, but it appears to be some kind of cross between a cat and a rat, though how that should come to be, I could not say."

"I'll wager you mean her ferret," Geoffrey replied sagely.

The maid's brow cleared. "A ferret, is it? Then you know about such things? Oh, please, sir, can't you tell me what to do? I'm new on staff, and I've never fed a creature before."

Might as well be of use to someone, Geoffrey thought as he nodded, pushing the door open wider. The maid drew back in relief, turning to lead him to a familiar handmade ornamental cage set on a table across from Allison's bed.

He couldn't help glancing about the room as he moved to the cage, curious about this bastion of female secrets. He was immediately disappointed. It was furnished much as his own room, with a four-poster bed hung in blue-and-green velvet, two wing-backed chairs near the marble fireplace, and a large wardrobe opposite. While his room also contained a highboy dresser, Allison's larger room held two such dressers and a dressing table with a mirror. The tops of all three were littered with female items like ribbons, silver-backed brushes, and jewelry cases. The only thing about the room that reminded him in any way of Allison was the ferret crouched in one corner of the cage, eyeing him balefully.

Geoffrey held out his hand to the maid. "Give me one of those pieces of meat."

The maid eagerly complied as Geoffrey pulled off his white glove to accept it with his left hand. With his right, he eased open the door to the cage.

The ferret hunkered lower. Geoffrey held out the tidbit to him, speaking gently.

"You remember me, don't you fellow? You should thank me for getting you out of that snare and setting you up in such fine digs. I'll wager you never ate so regularly or so well in all your life."

The ferret sniffed the air, eyeing the meat warily, but he refused to leave the safety of his corner. Geoffrey set the chunk on the sand at the bottom of the cage and drew back his hand. The ferret pounced greedily on the meat.

"There, you see?" Geoffrey proclaimed, grabbing two more pieces off the plate the awed maid held out to him. "Nothing to it." He tossed the pieces through the open door to the ferret's feet. The little animal tore into them as well. Pleased with himself, Geoffrey couldn't resist rubbing his hand over the soft fur. The ferret raised his head and nipped him.

"Damnation!" Geoffrey swore, yanking his hand out of the cage. The ferret took the opportunity of the open door and bolted. The maid screamed; the plate hit the hardwood floor with a shatter of china, and the ferret pelted for the open bedchamber door and catastrophe.

"Oh, no, you don't!" Geoffrey yelled, leaping after the creature. He could not be responsible for the ferret destroying yet another Munroe party. He scrambled into the hall, arms windmilling as he tried to keep his balance on the polished floor in his cursed evening pumps. Glancing wildly up and down the hall, he caught sight of a black-tipped tail disappearing under the window curtains near the door to the servants' stairs. He paused for a moment, sucking his sore hand and considering the best approach. Then he knelt and crept down the hall toward the curtains. The maid peered fearfully out of Allison's door, and he waved her back. He crouched before the curtains, poised to pounce on the small oblong lump he could see under them.

With pomp and proper ceremony, Perkins swung open the door from below stairs.

"Shut it!" Geoffrey hissed, watching for any movement from the curtains.

"I . . . I beg your pardon?" Perkins blustered.

"The door!" Geoffrey all but shouted. "We've got a ferret loose here, fellow! Shut the door unless you want it in the kitchen." Behind him he felt rather than saw the maid peer out the door again.

"If you have loosed Miss Allison's pet, sir," Perkins sniffed, "I daresay it will not go well for you."

Infuriated beyond reason, Geoffrey leapt to his feet. "And I can promise you it won't go well for you if you don't shut that damned door!"

The maid screamed, and Geoffrey whirled to tell her to be silent just in time to see a white streak of fur dash out from under the curtains, straight between Perkins's legs and down the open stairwell. He started forward after it, but—oblivious to the trouble he had caused— Perkins slowly shut the door.

"You idiot!" Geoffrey shouted.

Perkins backed away from his fury, right up against the door. "There is no need to get abusive, sir. I've done as you requested."

Geoffrey grabbed him by the shoulder and jerked him out of the way. "You've made a mess of it, rather. How many doors open off this stair?"

Perkins eyed him in silent reproach.

Geoffrey threw up his hands. "I don't have time for your foolishness! You there, maid, how many doors?"

The maid swallowed, glancing between him and Perkins. "Ju . . . just one, sir. It goes straight down to the kitchen, as you said."

Beyond her, other doors opened and he saw Alan and Bryce, Mrs. Munroe's abigail, poke out their heads. Bryce just as quickly pulled hers back in, but Alan, in full black evening wear, strode down the hall toward him. Geoffrey groaned.

"What, may I ask, is going on?" Alan queried with one expressive brown eyebrow raised.

To Geoffrey's surprise, Perkins immediately piped up. "This gentleman accosted me, Squire Pentercast. And he was abusive to Mary as well."

"Oh, fine, *now* you learn to do something quickly," Geoffrey fumed.

Alan frowned. "Care to explain, Geoff?"

"Frankly," Geoffrey told him, "we don't have time. Allison's ferret has escaped again and is headed for the kitchens. With the amount of traffic between stairs tonight, I don't have to tell you what kind of trouble he can cause. If we don't act now, Allison's come out will be the talk of London, for all the wrong reasons."

Five

Standing in the corner of her mother's bedchamber, Allison flinched as Bryce's comb snagged another curl. "Are you sure this is the latest style?" she asked with teeth clenched against the constant tug on her scalp.

In her mother's full-length pier glass, Allison watched the little abigail study the flaxen pile on top of Allison's head. Bryce's dark eyes looked thoughtful as she perched upon a stool to give her the height necessary to finish dressing Allison's hair. "Yes, Miss Allison. *A la Grèque*, just like in the *Lady's Monthly*. Isn't that what you wanted, madame?"

Mrs. Munroe moved from her inspection of her jewel case to pause before the mirror. She reached up to touch the conical pile with a languid gloved hand. "Exactly what I wanted, Bryce. Stop fidgeting, Allison. You'll wrinkle your gown."

Allison sighed and tried to relax. At least the whole ordeal was almost over. In less than two hours, she would be greeting her guests; and by this time tomorrow, it would all be a memory. She only had to endure two more tugs before Bryce proclaimed her done. Her mother handed the abigail the tiara. Allison swallowed as it was lowered over the braided bun.

"The Munroe diamonds. Oh, Mother, are you sure?"

Mrs. Munroe inclined her head. "Genevieve offered them for your use. Besides, you've worn them before."

Allison touched the cold stones with reverence. "Only once, when Genevieve invited the Pentercasts to dinner to make peace between the families."

Her mother turned away. "Let us hope this evening goes considerably better than that one did. From such a dismal beginning, I am continually amazed that Gen managed to attach the squire's regard."

As if to belie her mother's hopes, there came a scream and a crash from outside the room. Allison jumped. Her mother allowed a frown to crease her brow. "Whatever could that be?"

Allison turned toward the door, thankful for a chance to escape all this unwanted attention. "I'll go check."

"Stay where you are," her mother commanded with an imperious wave. Sighing, Allison settled back in front of the mirror.

"Now then, Bryce," her mother continued. "I think the diamond ear bobs as well, but only the single drop on the necklace. We don't want Allison to look over-done."

"Yes, madame," Bryce readily agreed, moving to lift the stones from their place in the box. Allison tried not to flinch again as the jewels were placed about her neck and at her ears. Looking in the mirror, she wasn't sure she liked the effect as much as her mother's nod of approval should indicate. The stones were lovely, but they seemed hard to her, cold, lifeless. "Couldn't I just take some of the tea roses we purchased to decorate the tables?" she ventured.

"If that was your attempt at a jest, it was inappropriate," her mother informed her. "Does that hem seem short to you, Bryce?"

"Where, madame?" Bryce cried, bending to inspect the full skirt of Allison's gold satin ball gown. At the time they had purchased the material, Allison had been sure it was the same lovely yellow as the roses; but under the candlelight in her mother's bedchamber, with the diamonds hung about her, it looked closer to a gold that seemed to her to very nearly clash with her pale hair. Her mother may have considered it in the best of taste, and it was difficult to argue that her mother's taste was nothing if not perfect, but Allison felt the word overdone was an apt description. She felt like some golden trophy awarded to the best horseman at a fox hunt.

"Walk about the room, Allison," her mother instructed, and with another heartfelt sigh, Allison complied. "No, Bryce, I was wrong. The skirt appears to be hanging correctly. Perhaps it was just the way Allison was standing."

From the hall came another scream. Allison froze in surprise. Her mother stiffened.

"Bryce, go see what that is all about," she murmured. Bryce scurried to poke her head out the door. Whatever she saw, it made her pale. She shut the door just as quickly and turned nervously to her mistress. "Nothing to be concerned about, madame. Squire Pentercast is investigating."

Mrs. Munroe nodded. "Very good. Now, Allison, stand in front of the mirror again, if you please. Something is not right."

Allison wasn't sure she wanted to know what was troubling her mother. It would only turn out to be some defect on her part—she was standing too straight; she was slouching; she was bowlegged; she was pigeon-toed; she had eaten too many chocolates and had put on weight since her fitting; she had not eaten enough and had lost weight since her fitting. She suddenly couldn't stand hearing another complaint, real or imaginary. "It's very rude of us to expect the squire to take care of everything," she declared, grabbing a length of skirt in one hand and striding to the door. "I will simply check to make sure everything is all right."

"Allison Ermintrude Munroe," her mother started, but Allison was out the door before she could finish the scold. Knowing it would take her mother some minutes to complete her own toilette before venturing out in company, she heaved another sigh, this one of pure relief. Then she peered down the hall to where it seemed that Geoffrey and Alan were having a hurried discussion, with Perkins glowering behind them.

"Geoffrey, Alan," she ventured. "Is anything amiss?"

Geoffrey whipped around to face her and froze. She could only hope that all the gentlemen at the ball had the same reaction he did. His brown eyes blinked; his firm jaw actually dropped, and she would not have been surprised to see drool forming at one corner of his open mouth. Perhaps her mother's taste in clothing was not so far off the mark at that.

Alan nodded at her and then at Geoffrey, then turned to hurry down the main stair. She couldn't help thinking they had just shared some sort of secret. She didn't much like secrets, unless she was part of them.

"Geoffrey?" she called again, picking up her long skirt to move toward him. "What's going on?"

"Nothing," Geoffrey began. He had to blink away the vision she presented to focus on the problem at hand. He offered her his best smile, but somehow he didn't think it looked as innocent as he intended.

Allison wasn't fooled. He was up to something; she was sure of it. Perkins confirmed it.

"This person," the butler interrupted quellingly, "has had the audacity to accost me."

Geoffrey glared at him. Perkins ignored him.

"Oh, honestly, Perkins." Allison shook her head. "I know Mr. Pentercast can be brash, but he would hardly accost you."

Perkins stood tall, staring over her head. "As you say, Miss Munroe. Will that be all?"

Much as Allison detested his manner, she could hardly keep him. With another shake of her head, she waved him on. He bowed curtly and turned to put his hand on the doorknob to the stair. Geoffrey's hand shot out to clamp down on his.

"Are you mad?" he hissed to Allison's surprise. "Can't you use the main stair?"

Perkins glared at him. "Certainly not! The main stair is for the family and their guests. It is most impertinent of me to use it on my duties."

"I'm sure," Geoffrey snarled, "that Mrs. Munroe would forgive you just this once."

"Mrs. Munroe might, but I would not. Now, stand aside, fellow."

"What is wrong with you two?" Allison demanded. "Geoffrey, let Perkins be about his business."

"Happy to," Geoffrey growled, "so long as his business does not involve this stair. Now, *you* move along, fellow or, by God, I'll accost you again."

Perkins removed his hand. "You see what I must contend with, Miss Munroe. I only hope you will inform your mother of this occurrence and that the fellow will be dealt with appropriately."

"Yes, yes, fine," Allison agreed, shooing him along with a wave of her hands. He held his head high and moved with measured tread toward the main stair. From below came a sudden crash and the sound of shouting.

"Geoffrey Pentercast," Allison declared, hands on hips. "I demand to know what is going on."

Several other voices joined the first. Mary peered around Allison's bedchamber door, pale and trembling. Genevieve poked her head out and Bryce's head reappeared. There was nothing for it. Geoffrey waved at them all cheerfully and drew Allison toward the main stair.

"If you must know," he whispered, "the ferret's escaped again."

Allison stared at him, endless possibilities dawning in horror. "Geoffrey, you didn't! Not tonight!"

"It wasn't my fault," he protested, the words sounding like a whine even to his ears. He hurried on. "We can discuss this all later. Right now, the important thing is to catch the little fellow before he can do any real damage." There came another crash, and he winced.

Allison hurried to the stairs. "I agree. Let's go."

Geoffrey caught her arm. "Wait. You can't go like that. Go back and reassure your sister and mother. Alan and I will take care of this."

"Somehow I doubt that," Allison informed him. "Think, Geoffrey. Pippin knows me better than anyone. I daresay he's more likely to come to me than any of you."

"Pippin?" Geoffrey couldn't help asking.

"Pip for short," Allison replied, shrugging him off and hurrying forward once more.

She gave Geoffrey no choice but to follow.

The sight that met their eyes as they peered into the kitchen a few minutes later was less than encouraging. Monsieur Philip, the short, round French chef her mother had hired for the Season, was cowering in the corner opposite them by the door to the rear yard, muttering imprecations in his native tongue. The scullery maid they had hired for the Season as well as the two hired for the ball had clambered up on the kitchen worktable in the center of the large, high-ceilinged room, knees pulled up to chins. Even though the oak table wobbled under their combined weight, their trembling provided glimpses of ankles and calves that the footmen would surely have found tantalizing, Geoffrey thought, under other circumstances. Unfortunately for them, the two footmen they had hired for the Season were busy banging on cupboard doors and whistling under chairs. The other two serving men hired for the ball were busily transferring the many delicacies for the midnight supper from the loaded sideboard beside the door into safe keeping in the pantry across the back of the room. They had yet to rescue the multi-tiered, many-pillared cake that sat on the sideboard across the room from where Allison and Geoffrey watched. Guarding the door to the pantry, broomstick at the ready, stood Alan.

He glanced up as they attempted to enter and waved the broomstick back and forth in warning. "No, you don't. Geoffrey, I thought you were coming down the back stair."

Geoffrey shrugged. "I was apprehended."

"It's my fault," Allison volunteered. "I thought I might be of assistance."

"As you can see, we have everything under control," Alan told her cheerfully.

One of the scullery maids yanked her legs up tighter and let out a warbling squeal, pointing across the kitchen toward Monsieur Philip, who blanched as white as the frosting on his cake. "There it goes!"

Although Allison was sure nothing had moved, Geoffrey darted toward the spot, only to collide with a footman intent on the same task. Arms and legs tangled, Geoffrey glowered in frustration at the man, who shrank under the gaze.

"No, there!" shouted another maid, and before Geoffrey could untangle himself, the other footman hurried toward the spot she indicated.

"I'll take no more chances," Alan declared. "You two—" He pointed to the serving men on the food relay. "—get that cake in here, now!"

The two uniformed servants hurriedly grabbed the

immense platter on which rested the cake, which Allison noticed was festooned with tiny yellow tea roses the exact shade of her gown. Balancing it between them, they moved with practiced ease toward the pantry door. With a sigh of relief, Geoffrey freed himself.

The back stair door opened for Perkins, and the ferret bolted into the room. The three maids screamed; Perkins froze; Geoffrey dove for the ferret with the footmen at his heels; Alan wielded his broom with purpose, and the beast made a flying leap for safety, straight up the cake.

"Pippin!" Allison cried in dismay and amazement. The serving men froze, obviously afraid to drop the cake and equally afraid not to. Geoffrey managed to stop himself—and the footmen against his back—before he, too, hit the cake. He scowled at the piece, trying to think of a way to remove the beast and still salvage the confection. Allison caught her breath as Pippin poked his furry, frosting-covered head out from behind a now lopsided layer, took a look at Geoffrey's face, and showed his fangs. Geoffrey shook his head, foreseeing his doom in the creature's beady black eyes.

The maids screamed in unison. Before Allison could hush them, Pippin scrambled out of the cake and down one of the serving men's legs. The poor fellow was so unnerved, he began hopping about, shaking his leg. The man on the other side of the cake made a manful effort to keep it upright, glaring at his partner. With a hopeless groan, Geoffrey made a snatch for the platter. The slick crystal slipped over his gloved fingers. The cake fell, exploding in all directions.

Geoffrey closed his eyes as cake and frosting showered him from head to foot. Pippin darted out of the wreckage, sliding across the marble floor toward Allison. Heart going out to the little creature, she knelt to stop his flight. Pippin scurried up into her arms. She cradled him close, crooning and stroking his heaving sides. Around her, everything seemed to go still.

"I have him," she called to the others, "safe and sound."

"Safe," Geoffrey replied, opening his eyes and striding to her side. "But hardly sound. Look at this place."

"The kitchen is the least of our worries," Alan told him, moving to join them. "Your gown will never pass your mother's approval now, Miss Allison."

Allison glanced down belatedly. Yellow frosting and tufts of white cake festooned her gown from hem to bosom. The diamond on her chest more closely resembled a frosted grape than the jewel it was. Her matching gloves were equally coated.

"Mais mon pièce de résistance!" the chef moaned, staring at the remains of the cake. "My masterpiece, ruined!"

Out in the entry, the clock struck eight.

Allison's eyes widened. "The guests will be here in one hour. We're doomed!"

Geoffrey grit his teeth. She thought he might agree with her, but her pride in him grew when he straightened his shoulders and replied, "No, we're not. You're going to have a come out if I have to bake a cake myself."

"The cake isn't the only thing we'll have to manufacture," Alan pointed out.

Allison glanced down at her dress again. "Don't worry about the dress. I'll change in my room and Mother won't know until she sees me at the receiving line. By then, it will be too late." She hugged Pippin to her and turned to go; then, feeling Geoffrey's eyes on her, she couldn't resist turning back. "Thank you, Geoffrey, for not giving up."

He scowled at her and she decided to escape before he could say anything to spoil his heroism.

Of course, nothing she owned compared to the

golden-yellow dress. Mary had just finished setting the
room to rights when Allison entered and, obviously feeling guilty for Pippin's escape, was only too happy to
help Allison search through the wardrobe. In the end,
she chose a blue satin gown the color of her eyes with
a silver net overskirt. When Mary hung the diamond
necklace, which she had hurriedly rinsed off in the ba-
sin, about Allison's neck, the stones gleamed just as
blue. Somehow, they seemed less cold to her. Satisfied,
she hurried downstairs to join her family.

Her mother's eyes glittered more coldly than the diamonds when she saw Allison's outfit. Luckily, the first
guests were arriving, and she could say nothing in front
of so many people. Allison bobbed and curtseyed and
nodded as appropriate as each of their guests was introduced, all the while keeping one ear toward the back
stairs and the kitchen. She found it impossible to hide
her disappointment when the last guest had been ush-
ered in and still Geoffrey had not appeared.

"May I escort you on your night, Miss Allison?" Alan
asked beside her. When she sighed, he frowned. Catching her mother's barely raised eyebrow, Allison pasted
on a smile.

"How very thoughtful of you, squire," she replied and
her mother nodded. Together they made their way into
the ballroom.

She expected Alan to lead her out for the first dance,
which the string quartet was even now launching into.
To her surprise, he relinquished her hand to the Marquis DeGuis, who bowed with the same formality he had
shown in the entryway.

"Miss Munroe, will you do me the honor of this
dance?" he inquired.

She was tempted to accept him. In his formal evening
black, he was a magnificent sight, all black-and-white
contrasts from his jet-black hair to the white of the cra-

vat to the black of his coat and breeches and the white
stockings. She had never seen his smile warmer. But the
hero of the hour was Geoffrey Pentercast and loyalty
demanded that she wait. She glanced again toward the
entryway, earning another look from her mother. Even
if Geoffrey appeared, she realized, she would have to
take her first dance with the most senior gentleman at
the ball. The marquis's rank made him the obvious
choice. She curtseyed. "Thank you. I would be delighted."

He gave her his arm and escorted her to the set that
was forming. It was one of the most common of dances,
"Hole in the Wall," and she wished her mother would
have thought of something more original for the first
dance. Still, the marquis moved through the paces with
practiced ease, comporting himself with her and the
other lady of their quartet with equal grace. Even when
they stood out at either end of the set, his conversation
was about the commonplace and ordinary.

It was like every other ball she had attended since
arriving in London. Somehow, she had always thought
hers would be special. As she danced down the line of
couples or promenaded with Grace around the sides of
the room, however, she realized why the night was so
disappointing.

It simply wasn't her ball. She would never have chosen the diamonds to go with the golden dress. While
the string quartet was elegant, she would have chosen
more lively dances than the ones they minced through.
Besides Grace, Lady Janice, and Margaret, there was no
one in attendance that she would have been pleased to
call friend. All the anticipation, all the anxiety, for what?
She'd have much rather been playing penny loo with
Geoffrey in the kitchen.

And as soon as she could make her escape, she stole
away to do just that.

Six

As it turned out, the cake was the least of Geoffrey's worries that night. A pointed suggestion was enough to get the French chef to make petit fours from the remains. Among the other delicacies Alan had managed to save in the pantry, the lack of a centerpiece was not noticeable, at least to Geoffrey's admittedly unsophisticated eye.

He hoped the lack of his presence at the ball was equally unnoticed. It wasn't as if he were needed in the kitchen. Mrs. Munroe had hired plenty of servants to augment their already considerable staff. As soon as Allison, Pippin, and Alan left, they all scurried about their duties for the impending party while Perkins wandered about in silence. At first Geoffrey thought he was trying to act as if he were above the chaos around him, but then he noticed that the man could direct his staff with no more than a pointed look to send them on their way. Some of his minions cast Geoffrey surreptitious glances, as if they wondered why he stood glowering in the corner. Most simply ignored him, focusing on the task at hand. Several times he noticed the French chef on the verge of asking his help in some matter; but each time the little man encountered Geoffrey's gaze, he swallowed and hurried on. Perkins ignored him and left to continue his duties with the arriving guests.

Geoffrey knew his mother would have had apoplexy

if she had known he was using the excuse of the ferret's mess, which was cleaned up in miraculously short time with no help from him, to hide away in the nether regions of the house. Even when he realized he wasn't needed, he felt it his duty to make sure nothing else went wrong to spoil Allison's special evening. Besides, hiding in the kitchen was surely safer than confronting Mrs. Munroe. He wished he could count on her renowned calm, but he was fairly sure that even she had to be gnashing her teeth over the change in plans. Best he just stay out of her way.

Unfortunately, hiding in the kitchen kept him from seeing how Allison was faring. He wondered whether Alan had been given the honor of escorting her out for the first dance. He wondered whether the gown she had found to wear called attention to her bosom the way the yellow-gold dress had done. Most of all he wondered whether the reportedly dashing Marquis DeGuis had been similarly appreciative of her many charms. As each moment passed, he found more and more things to wonder about. His concerns must have shown on his face, for he suddenly noticed that the serving staff were going out of their way to bypass his corner. This ridiculous fear did nothing to assuage his growing anger at himself, at Allison's mother, at Pippin, and at everyone who was out in the ballroom enjoying themselves. By the time the last tidbit had been sent out for the midnight supper, with most of the servants accompanying it in some capacity and the chef retiring from a case of nerves, he was clenching his fists at his side and wishing someone would give him an excuse to start a fight. When the door from the ground floor opened moments later, he snarled "oh what now" before he even looked to see which of the servants had forgotten something.

"Is that any way to greet your rescuer?" Allison laughed from the doorway.

Geoffrey jumped to his feet from where he slouched against the far wall. He found he liked the light-blue satin dress she had chosen to replace the gold one. This dress had more flounces and made her look younger and happier. Her radiant appearance only made him realize how dingy he must look. White cake still festooned the front of his coat and dribbled down his breeches. His evening pumps were thick with frosting. He wondered where else the cake might have lodged that he didn't notice at the moment. His one consolation was that in taking the brunt of the explosion, he had spared the servants from trying to find matching livery to replace any damaged ones.

Allison grinned at him. There was nothing even remotely perfect or stuffy about his frosting-dabbed attire. He had never looked better to her. "You're obviously enjoying yourself down here," she teased, "so perhaps I should return to the ball."

Geoffrey grinned back, pleased to see her so happy. "Perhaps you should at that, before you ruin another dress. It is your party, after all. How goes it?"

Allison made a face. "Tedious beyond words. Honestly, Geoffrey, I've never been so disappointed in all my life. To think how much I believed I was missing!"

"As bad as all that?" Geoffrey asked, surprised as well.

"Worse," Allison assured him. "I can see now I should have taken a stronger stance on those invitations. Grace, Margaret, Lady Janice, and I can barely find enough partners to fill the dance floor. These may be the cream of London society, but they seem like nothing but the veriest of stuffed dolls."

"So much for taking London by storm." Geoffrey laughed. "Are you ready to give up and come home?"

She knew he was teasing, but she refused to give in anyway. "Never!" she declared vehemently. "I still have to convince Mother that I'm an adult. Do you know she refused to let the musicians play a waltz when I asked?"

"Horrors!" Geoffrey cried in mock dismay, enjoying the fire in her eye and the way she jutted out her chin defiantly. "A little too wicked for the proper London family, eh?"

Allison tossed her head. "Everyone who is anyone dances the waltz. Lady Jersey says so!"

"Really?" He couldn't let such a moment pass. He stripped off his soiled coat, tossing it on the table. "I surely wouldn't want this evening to be a total disappointment for you. By all means, let us waltz."

Allison stared at him, sure he was still teasing. He held out his arms encouragingly. She looked dubious. "You cannot be serious."

"Why not? This is one place your mother will surely not invade tonight. And we'd better be quick about it or the servants will invade. That supper will not last forever." He sketched a bow, lowering his head so she would not see the hope in his eyes. "Miss Munroe, may I have the honor of this dance?"

Her laugh bubbled up, spoiling the seriousness of her answering curtsey. "Mr. Pentercast, I would be delighted."

He slipped his arms about her slender waist, careful to keep her dress from touching his stained breeches, even though all of him shouted to hold her close. Humming, he led her about the room in what he hoped was something approaching the dance he had only seen performed once before.

Allison's heart was beating much faster than the slow, careful movements would imply. She didn't want to think why. This was far more fun than the ball, and not a little frightening, if in a heady sort of way. Geoffrey's gaze was warm and soft, bathing her in appreciation and pleasure. She could have danced like this the entire night.

They spun about the worktable and past the fire, setting her dress and diamonds glimmering in the light. Geoffrey gazed down into Allison's eyes, which sparkled like twin jewels, dimming the glow from the diamonds. He felt his breath coming fast, and somehow he didn't think it was because of the dance. He leaned forward and whispered into her ear, "See, moonling, isn't this better than a crowded ballroom?"

"Allison Ermintrude Munroe!"

Geoffrey froze, and Allison jerked to a stop, blanching. He was afraid to turn, knowing Mrs. Munroe would surely throw him out this very night. Allison recognized the voice and sagged with relief. Turning, he saw Genevieve standing in the doorway, hands on the hips of her rose satin ball gown, a scowl on her pretty face.

"Oh, Gen," Allison sighed, "it's only you."

"Yes, and you can be quite glad of that," Gen replied firmly, marching into the room. "Though you can be certain that the moment Mother realizes you have abandoned your guests for the kitchen, she will be after you as well."

"It's my fault." Geoffrey sighed, more from disappointment that the moment was over than from any regret.

Genevieve turned her scowl at him. "Do not make matters any worse for yourself, Geoffrey. You are in quite enough trouble as it is."

"You needn't lash into him simply because he's the only one at this ball who knows how to have fun," Allison defended him loyally.

"And don't make matters worse for yourself either, Allison," Genevieve retorted. "Quickly now, before Mother realizes where you've gone. The only reason she isn't looking for you is that she thinks you're promenading with Lord DeGuis."

All thoughts of loyalty fled at the sound of his rival's name. "Does she, indeed?" Geoffrey snarled.

Allison frowned at him. "As I am clearly not promenading with Lord DeGuis, I see no reason for you to be testy." Her frown deepened as she realized the import of his actions. He was jealous of all things, as if he couldn't tell what the last few minutes meant to her. Annoyed, she stepped away from him. "In fact, I see no reason for you to be testy either way. You are quite right, Genevieve; this kitchen is even more tiresome than my ball. Let us return to our guests."

Geoffrey stood by the sideboard, fuming, but powerless to stop her.

Allison returned to the ball, but she found it even less enjoyable. After her warm reception in the kitchen, her guests seemed all the more stuffy. By one o'clock, she was ready to send them all home; by two she was ready to sneak upstairs to bed and leave them to whatever it was they were finding amusing about the entire affair. It wasn't until nearly three-thirty that she bid the last guest adieu and turned to find her mother and sister eyeing her.

"I do not want to know what occurred," her mother intoned, "to cause you to have to change your gown from the one Bryce and I worked so hard to fit for you. I do not want to know why you left your guests in the middle of a ball in your honor. I simply want that man out of my house, tonight if possible. However, I shall settle on tomorrow morning. Goodnight, Genevieve."

She climbed the stairs, iron-gray head high, spine straight, skirt of her lavender ball gown trailing behind her in a perfect line. Perkins, who had been standing sentry nearby, moved slowly toward the back of the

house. Allison closed her eyes and sighed, failure wash-
ing over her.

"I'll send Alan for Geoffrey," Gen offered, linking an
arm in hers. "Let's go to the library. I think Perkins
had a fire there for some of the older guests to escape
the merriment."

"What merriment?" Allison couldn't help asking de-
jectedly.

Upstairs, Geoffrey was nearly at his wit's end. Allison's
defection had not been the last of his trials that night.
After he had calmed himself, he had realized that his
best defense against this absurd jealousy was to attend
the rest of the ball himself. Surely, he had reasoned,
Mrs. Munroe would have relaxed by now. From Allison's
description of the staid ball, the widow could only be
pleased. Besides, Allison couldn't very well promenade
with the Marquis DeGuis if she were promenading with
him instead. Unfortunately, his evening clothes were
soiled beyond any repair he could make and he had no
others with him. He had retired upstairs to ransack
Alan's wardrobe, but his brother had packed lightly and
was obviously wearing the only set of appropriate ap-
parel. Mrs. Munroe kept all the footmen in navy livery,
so he couldn't easily borrow their coats or breeches; and
he had cringed at the thought of approaching Perkins.
In the end, all he could do was stalk about his borrowed
room in Alan's dressing gown and mutter curses at everyone and everything.

For all Allison had claimed the ball to be tiresome,
it had taken abominably long to break up in Geoffrey's
opinion. He was actually considering loosing the ferret
again when he began to hear carriages pulling away below. A short time later, there was a rap on his door and
Alan looked in.

"It's a good thing you're still awake," he told Geoffrey. "My wife tells me that she cannot sleep unless we've had a full accounting from you."

Geoffrey sighed. "Haven't I atoned enough by missing the ball?"

"Apparently not," Alan quipped. He held open the door for him. "Downstairs, if you please, in the library."

Geoffrey shook his head but moved to comply.

He was only slightly relieved when he saw that Allison was with her sister in the room. Like the other rooms in the rented house, it did little to reflect its owners, unless perhaps it was the widow Munroe. He somehow found it hard to imagine Allison reading any of the thick, leather-bound volumes that clung to the glass-fronted bookshelves lining the walls in orderly fashion— just as the four leather armchairs were arranged in perfect square in the center of the room.

He wanted nothing more than to confront Allison and demand to know whether the marquis had proposed, but Genevieve was frowning at him from the chair next to her sister and he decided the safest place for him was the farthest place from her. Accordingly, he stopped to eye the bookshelves just inside the room.

Allison regarded him, wondering what she could do to change what was going to happen. She didn't want them to send him home. He had been the only breath of fresh air in her entire suffocatingly stuffy ball. He shouldn't be penalized for that. Geoffrey could feel Allison watching him and couldn't resist another look. There was sadness in her eyes, and he hoped that didn't mean he had spoiled her ball after all.

"I do not see why we need to do this, Genevieve," she said. "The ball was a success according to everyone with whom I talked. Even Mother seemed pleased, until the end."

So, things had gone well after all. He couldn't help but feel pleased. Genevieve seemed less impressed.

"Mother may have been pleased about what was left of her ball," Genevieve replied, "but as she noted, she will find Geoffrey's company even more difficult to accept after this. Even though we are returning to Somerset soon, I do not think we can overlook this incident."

Allison shook her head vehemently, even as Geoffrey frowned at the superior tone. "But, Gen, this is no different from the pranks Geoffrey used to play when we were children. I remember him dropping a frog on the pages of our books while we studied, yanking my ribbons out of my hair to use as fishing line, and throwing apples at me from his side of the wall."

"As I recall," Genevieve mused, "you made a pet of the frog, got Chimes to settle the fish you caught with the ribbons into the Abbey pond, and refused to share the pie Annie cooked from the apples."

Geoffrey hid a grin.

"My point exactly," Allison declared. "All those things turned out well, just as tonight did. I fail to see why Geoffrey must be made to suffer any more than he already has."

"From what I observed, Geoffrey has hardly suffered at all," Genevieve replied, frowning at her sister and sending a chill up Geoffrey's spine with her coldness. "And you know how Mother feels. He cannot get out of this one so easily, Allison. He is long past the age of childish pranks, or should be. You know as well as I do that Mother has a fairly rigid set of standards to which she expects everyone to adhere."

Geoffrey caught Allison's gaze and smiled in sympathy.

"Yes, Gen," Allison murmured. "I know. But while you and I might try to live up to them, I find it insupportable that she should have a right to enforce them on others."

Genevieve raised an eyebrow. "Insupportable? Allison, I think you should remember your place."

Geoffrey winced.

Allison reacted exactly as he would have expected her to. "My place!" she cried, leaping to her feet. "Do you know how much you sound like Mother? 'Allison, moderate your tone.' 'Allison, such opinions are not suitable for a proper young lady.' 'Allison, silence is a virtue.' Do my thoughts, my feelings, count for nothing in this family?"

"Of course they count for something," Genevieve protested, clearly abashed. "I know what it means to fight for what you believe in, Allison. I meant only that it is our duty to respect Mother's wishes while we live under her roof whenever possible, however difficult that may be at times."

"If it comes to that," Allison sniffed, returning to her seat, "this roof belongs to Alan."

Alan acknowledged her remark with a nod. "That may be true from a financial sense, Miss Allison. But I have always made it clear that this is your mother's home. I agree with Genevieve that we should respect your mother's wishes. Besides, I've been considering what to do about Geoffrey for some time."

Geoffrey stirred, stung, and abandoned his attempt to remain casual. "I see Allison is not the only one to be accorded little respect. I was not aware I had asked for your help, brother."

"Perhaps not in so many words," Alan replied. "But every time you pull one of these pranks, I am reminded that I have not done my duty by you."

"Am I such a monster," Geoffrey murmured, shaken by Alan's words, "that you are so ashamed of me?"

Allison cried out at his pain, but Gen hushed her.

"Let us say," Alan told him firmly, "that your behavior lacks what I would expect from a gentleman."

Geoffrey grit his teeth, feeling as if he'd been punched in the gut. Even last winter, when the entire village had been sure he had committed several crimes, Alan had stood by him. To have that support taken away because of a ferret seemed cruel in the extreme. "Then do whatever you wish with me," he managed, "since I obviously have no worth."

"The punishment should fit the crime, I've always thought," Alan mused.

Allison leapt to her feet again. "I know! You claim Geoffrey is uncivil. Let him stay here, in London, to learn to be a gentleman."

"Thank you for that, moonling," Geoffrey murmured, not able to take his eyes from his brother's face.

"No," Alan replied. "That would hardly suit your mother, Miss Allison, and it will not help Geoffrey, as I cannot stay to keep an eye on him. No, it seems to me that Geoffrey will be best served if he can be made to face his faults."

"And you don't think pointing them out to me before an audience sufficient?" Geoffrey growled.

"Not nearly enough. I have in mind to give you a mirror, Geoffrey, a man so uncivil, as Miss Allison calls it, that the entire village of Wenwood shuns him."

"Oh, Alan, no!" Genevieve cried in obvious realization of his intent.

Allison sank back on to the chair with similar understanding. "You would not be so cruel!"

Even Geoffrey had an inkling of his brother's plan. "You cannot mean whom I think you mean," he told Alan.

Alan glanced from one to the other. "Yes, I can, Geoffrey. You leave me no choice but to send you to the most difficult, cantankerous, uncivil man it has ever

been my dubious honor to know. If I can convince him
to take you, you will spend the rest of the spring and
summer with Enoch McCreedy."

Seven

Allison stood on the steps of the London town house, shivering in the pale light of morning although her blue pelisse should have kept her warm and the day promised to be bright. The creak of harness on the waiting team of horses sounded melancholy to her, and it seemed rather fitting that the coach hired to return Geoffrey to the country was black. She had not been so miserable since she had lost her father.

Alan leaned back out of the carriage, having just finished tucking lap robes around her sister. He glanced impatiently at the house, then focused on Allison. "Where is he?"

"You cannot blame him," Allison replied with a sniff, "if he isn't eager to leave this morning."

Alan sighed. "Miss Allison, you must believe me that this is for his own good. If Enoch can help knock off his rough edges, Geoffrey just might find his own way in the world. It is long past time he learned how." He grinned suddenly, reminding her of his brother. "And you may like him better as well."

Allison refused to return his smile. "Some people would say they like him well enough right now," she retorted.

"And glad I am for that," Geoffrey put in, appearing in the doorway. Despite the bantering tone, he looked more dismal than she had ever seen him. His curly hair

stuck out at all angles, and there were bags under his
eyes as if he had not slept well. His chin seemed even
more determined than usual. He brightened as he
looked her over, then sobered again as his gaze swept
over the waiting coach.

"Your bags are already aboard," Alan called. "Say
your farewells, and let's be off."

Allison caught her breath. She had been trying to
prepare herself for this moment since Alan had made
his announcement in the library only a few hours ago.
That little amount of time had forced her to confront
how she felt about Geoffrey. After thinking about him
for weeks, it had seemed like nothing short of a miracle
that he had appeared in London. He had hinted of
marriage, of course; but she told herself she couldn't
take that too seriously. She thought him handsome; she
thought him clever; she thought him enjoyable company, but she was entirely too comfortable with him to
think of him as a husband.

Besides, she knew Geoffrey, sometimes better than he
knew himself. For all that she liked to think he found
her equally attractive and clever, the truth was that she
was one of his dearest, closest friends. She had never
seen a couple who married from friendship. Certainly
her mother and father had had little in common. And
Genevieve and Alan had started out as bitter enemies.
No, marriage to Geoffrey was too easy. If there were
anything good to be said for this sojourn with Enoch
McCreedy, it was that it would give Geoffrey and her
time to think over their feelings.

Geoffrey scowled at Alan and turned to her. She
smiled hopefully, praying he wouldn't notice the red
rims of her eyes or the pallor of her cheeks. All night
she had worried about what Enoch McCreedy might do
to him. The pariah of the village, he insulted everyone
who came to his farm to buy the horses that were his

one claim to decency. He went out of his way to find fault in everyone and everything. It was said he drowned kittens for fun. She shuddered just thinking about spending time with the man, but she knew she mustn't let Geoffrey know of her fears.

Unfortunately, her face must have given her away, for he reached out to tuck a stray curl back inside the rim of her straw bonnet and murmured, "I hope you weren't crying because of me."

"Why else would I be crying?" she demanded. His lopsided smile only fueled her fire. "Will you be serious? Promise me you'll be careful."

"As careful as need be," Geoffrey allowed. "Just think, when I return, we'll have all the more stories to tell each other."

She should have responded as lightheartedly as he did, but she found she couldn't. "I've heard entirely too many stories about Enoch McCreedy."

"I've heard the same stories." He shrugged. "But perhaps they're only that—stories fabricated to frighten children into obedience. I'm not a child, Allison, no matter what some people seem to think. I don't frighten easily."

"I don't understand you," she hissed, aware of the eyes watching her from the carriage. "Refuse them. Stand your ground. You're nearly four years older than I am. Surely twenty-two is old enough to make its own decisions."

"A man doesn't reach his majority until twenty-five," Geoffrey reminded her. "Besides, defying my brother, and your sister and mother, is hardly likely to get them to look kindly on my suit."

Allison felt the color surge to her cheeks. "Oh, come now, Geoffrey," she said in what she hoped was a teasing tone. "You don't honestly expect me to believe you truly want to marry me."

He returned her stare boldly. "Of course I want to marry you, moonling. This isn't the time or place of my choosing, but I hope you know there's no other girl in the world for me."

"Oh, Geoffrey," she managed. She was going to cry again; she could feel it. She swallowed instead, unsure what to say in return. She couldn't very well promise undying devotion, not when she wasn't sure she loved him. It would be unkind to let him think she agreed to his suit. But she couldn't seem to open her mouth to tell him so.

"Normally, I'd say hang the lot of them," Geoffrey continued, "and we'd simply elope. But we need their good graces if we are to have the life I'd want for you."

She heard the coachman cough and wished them all to perdition. "Listen, Geoffrey, you mustn't say such things, not now. You're the dearest friend I have in all the world, but I'm not ready to marry. I told you, I need this Season to ensure my family understands that I've grown up."

Alan added his cough to that of the driver. Geoffrey felt the mounting pressure as well. He caught her hand and pressed it fervently to his lips. Allison was surprised to feel herself begin to tremble at the sweet pressure of his kiss.

"Have your Season, Allison," he murmured. "I'll bide my time with McCreedy as Alan has commanded. When you return home at the end of the summer, we'll talk." He grinned at her and her heart somersaulted. "And I'll stand my ground then, I promise."

Allison could only nod, feeling tears pooling behind her eyes once more. She ought to be calm. She ought to be as proper and elegant as her sister and mother. She ought to send him off with a curtsey and a polite smile. For a second, she considered doing all those things, but only for a second. Then she threw her arms around him and hugged him close. "Oh, Geoffrey, how I'll miss you!"

She felt his arms come around her and heard his voice whisper in her ear. "I'll miss you too, moonling. More than you can know. Wait for me."

She nodded, gulping back tears. Beside the carriage, Alan cleared his throat rather loudly. Geoffrey let go of her, offered her one last grin, and ran down the steps to the coach. She waved until they were lost in the early-morning traffic. Then she returned to the house with heavy steps. The four remaining months they intended to stay in London seemed like eternity. She only hoped Geoffrey would find it easier than she feared. And she hoped she would make it through her Season.

Somehow Allison survived. She thought of Geoffrey just as often as she had before he was ostracized; and there were times when she was cavorting about the ball-room floor, at other balls far more interesting than her own, when she felt guilty for enjoying herself. She started several letters to him, only to put them aside before finishing. Her mother would hardly allow her to post them herself, and Perkins would never have carried them without tattling. She did manage to convince one of the footmen to carry an encouraging note; but as he was threatened with sacking for neglecting his other duties for his good deed, she was sure no one else would volunteer. In the end, she determined that the best she could do for Geoffrey was to get through the Season and return to Wenwood. Surely she could convince Alan to commute Geoffrey's sentence if she were there to plead his case personally.

By the end of August, she was more than ready to return to the cool stone corridors of Wenwood Abbey. The last ball, celebrating one of Wellington's victories, was over. All that remained was to finish packing and remand the staff to the agency from which they had hired them. When Perkins came to inform her that her mother wished to speak to her, she had to restrain herself from gloating at the thought that this would be one of the last times she would have to deal with him.

Her mother was seated at the Sheridan writing table when Allison entered the sitting room. Her dove-gray gown stood out against flowers on the other surfaces. Mrs. Munroe looked up from her writing and nodded toward the nearest armchair. Allison sat, tilting her head to catch a glimpse of the list she was sure her mother must be making of the tasks remaining before their departure. To her surprise, she saw that her mother was responding to an invitation.

"Are we to have another dinner party?" Allison couldn't help sighing, plucking at the folds of her green sprigged-muslin gown.

Her mother pursed her lips. "A lady is always ready to entertain as needed, Allison. However, this is not for a dinner party. I have decided to invite one of your friends to join us at Wenwood."

Allison brightened. "Grace?"

"No, not Miss Dunsworthy," her mother replied. "And not Lady Janice or your dreadful cousin Margaret."

Allison made a face at her mother's censorship. "I find Margaret's company invigorating, even if she doesn't have the social grace of some. But if not those you mentioned, then whom?"

"I have invited the Marquis DeGuis," her mother replied calmly.

Allison stared at her, not sure what to think. Her heart leapt at the chance to spend some time alone with the man and perhaps get to know him better, but it would be difficult to free Geoffrey if she were busy entertaining a visitor. "Oh, Mother, why?"

Her mother raised an eyebrow. "Is there some reason I should not?"

"One rather large one and a great many small ones," Allison maintained. "If you invite only him, aren't you concerned what the gossips will say?"

"What can gossips say that could possibly be of interest?" her mother sniffed.

"They will say I've set my cap for him," Allison told her. "And while that may not bother you, it bothers me a great deal."

Her mother avoided her eyes, dipping her quill carefully in the inkwell. "And haven't you set your cap for him?"

"Mother!" Allison gasped, stunned by the very idea. "Good heavens, no!"

Her mother paused in her writing. "Oh? Why not? I understand he is all the rage with the young ladies of the *ton.*"

"I well imagine he is," Allison allowed. "All the more reason for me not to attempt to attach his interest. Truly, Mother, you should not invite him to the Abbey. He will be bored beyond tears there. He does not strike me as caring to live anywhere but London."

"He has already written to say he finds the idea of a country sojourn delightful," her mother replied.

Allison did not take time to disagree. "He is used to the Social whirl. Surely he will find the company of two women stifling in the extreme."

"He will have the squire's company, I am assured, as well as Genevieve's, at least for a time. And he certainly has not complained of your presence in the past."

Allison gave up on logic. "But, Mother," she all but wailed, "he isn't any fun!"

Her mother shook her head with a martyred sigh.

"There are more important things in life than fun, Allison. I had hoped you might have learned that this Season. However, your attitude only confirms the wisdom of my making this decision myself."

Allison wanted to shout in vexation. An entire six months in London and she still couldn't be counted on in her mother's eyes to select a guest! With great difficulty, she took a deep breath and forced herself to sit calmly beside her mother.

"I wish you would not take such a tone with me, Mother," she murmured with ladylike restraint. "You began this conversation by saying you wished to invite one of my friends to visit the Abbey. I merely wanted to point out that the Marquis DeGuis is not a particular friend."

Her mother gazed at her almost distractedly and Allison wondered whether her sudden change of attitude was only serving to confuse her mother. "Have you taken him in dislike, then?" her mother managed with a strangled voice.

Allison wanted to answer yes, but knew it was not the truth. The marquis had been relatively pleasant company, even if he didn't know how to talk beyond the commonplace; and one simply could not complain about his looks, demeanor, or wardrobe. "Not dislike," she hedged. "He has been very kind. Perhaps I simply never got to know him."

Her mother seemed to relax, turning back to her writing. "All the more reason to invite him to the country, where you can spend more time with him."

Allison grit her teeth, but kept a pleasant smile on her face. "I do not think that is necessary, Mother. If I wish to get to know the marquis better, I can always do that next Season."

Her mother sighed, long fingers going to squeeze the bridge of her nose. She closed her eyes and sighed again.

"Mother?" Allison swallowed, alarm rising at this unfamiliar display of emotion. "Are you all right?"

"You are a sad trial to me, Allison," her mother murmured without opening her eyes, further depressing Allison's spirits. "You are entirely too like your father—prone to odd humors and irrational whims. I truly thought you would outgrow them."

Allison struggled with the weight of guilt the words placed on her shoulders. "I always admired Father. Many people did. I realize his approach to life was different from yours, but does that make it wrong?"

"For a man of adequate means, many things are possible," her mother replied, opening her eyes at last. "You are a woman, Allison; and despite the squire's generosity, you are a woman of limited means. You do not have the luxury of throwing away what is offered you." She squared her shoulders and met Allison's gaze. The determination in the gray-blue eyes only served to unnerve Allison further.

"The Marquis DeGuis has requested my permission to marry you. I have agreed."

Allison stared at her, feeling the blood drain from her face. "You did *what*?" she whispered.

The determination in her mother's face increased. "You will marry him before Parliament opens in November. I have already arranged for the gown, the flowers, and the church. He is an excellent match, Allison. He will make a fine husband."

"For someone. Not for me." She gasped in a breath. "You cannot do this to me, Mother. You cannot simply choose a future for me and force me to fit it. I'm not a dress pattern that you can alter to suit your whim."

Her mother returned to the note in dismissal. "There is nothing more to be said on the matter. The announcement will appear in the *Times* as soon as the marquis deems proper. I have already written to tell Genevieve the news."

"You told Gen?" Allison rasped, knowing how swiftly such news would travel in the country. By now, the entire village would know. And sooner or later, word would reach Geoffrey.

"I told Genevieve and the Reverend Wellfordhouse," her mother replied calmly, as if somehow she had failed to notice the world crashing down around her daughter. "The marquis would have preferred a London wedding, but Genevieve will be unable to travel by then and I must have her at the wedding. We could have postponed the event until after the baby was born, I suppose, but I had promised the marquis you would wed before the year was out. And in any event, he will want to return for the start of Parliament."

"No," Allison whispered, rising even as her voice rose with each repetition of the word. "No, no, no. I will not marry the marquis, not in Wenwood, not in London, not in November, not ever!"

"Allison," her mother said quellingly, "moderate your tone."

"No!" Allison shouted. "I will shout; I will jump; I will ride Rotten Row in my chemise if that will make you listen. This is my *life*, Mother. You cannot dictate whom I will wed."

"The subject is closed," her mother replied, dusting sand across the ink on the note. "We will be leaving for the country in a week's time. You may wish to speak to Mary about her future. No doubt the marquis has any number of servants, but I believe it is customary for the new wife to bring her own abigail with her. If Mary has given good service, you may wish to offer her the position. I will be offering one to Perkins."

Allison said every word with determination. "There is no position to offer Mary. I will pack; I will return to the Abbey. But under no circumstances will I marry the Marquis DeGuis. And now, madame, you may consider the subject closed."

Eight

Wentwood, Somerset
Summer's End, 1813

"Easy." Geoffrey soothed the panting mare, hoping her struggles wouldn't awaken the sleeping grooms at the back of the stables. "Easy now, girl. Just a little longer."

"It's no good," Enoch McCreedy grumbled, wiping sweat from his brow with the sleeve of his worn lawn shirt. "I knew when that stallion of Henry Jarvis's broke through the fence last summer there'd be trouble. The foal's too big for her."

Geoffrey glanced up at the most cantankerous man in Wenwood. After four months of nearly constant company, he recognized that Enoch's set jaw and heavy-browed frown were more from concern than dismissal of the mare's condition. He glanced down again at the lathered bay lying beside him. "She's your best mare. Is there no way to save her?"

Enoch folded long legs to crouch beside him in the straw of the stall. Large hands reached out to stroke the heaving sides. "Maybe. It's all up to her."

As if in answer, the normally docile mare reared back her head and attempted to take a bite out of Enoch's arm. He jerked back and rose, craggy frame stiff in the hastily donned, patched tweed trousers. "She doesn't want *my* help. That's clear."

Geoffrey murmured soothingly, and the horse lowered her head, panting. "Still, I knew when I heard her shuffling about out here, her time was near. It made me glad you had me sleep in the back room with the grooms and stable boys. Perhaps she'll let me help. Tell me what to do, Enoch."

"It won't be easy," Enoch grumbled, running a hand back through his already disheveled coal-black hair. Geoffrey could feel the knowing blue eyes boring into his back. "Could take a couple of hours. You won't get any more sleep tonight."

"I'll manage," Geoffrey replied, glancing back with a grin.

Enoch nodded. "All right, then. Here's what we do."

Four hours and twenty buckets of sweat later, Geoffrey Pentercast helped the foal to stand. It was the same warm bay as her mother, though the black patch down her nose spoke of her father as well. Coat still matted with birth fluid, she teetered over to her mother to demand her first drink. Geoffrey leaned against the stall door and sighed with relief, weariness, and elation.

Enoch nodded toward the foal. "This is only the beginning of her struggles. Born this late, she'll likely not live to see the spring."

"She'll make it," Geoffrey predicted. "She's got spirit. You can see it."

"Well, I don't want the extra work," Enoch maintained. "If you think she's so fine, she's yours."

Geoffrey straightened, staring at the man. "Do you mean that?"

Enoch scowled at him, long hooked nose formidable. "Am I known to say things I don't mean?"

"No." Geoffrey laughed, offering his hand, which

Enoch accepted with a telltale twinkle in his blue eyes. "Thank you, Enoch. I'll take good care of her."

"As to that," Enoch growled, turning away, "you'd better speak to your brother. You'll be going home soon. He'll have to decide whether he has room for the foal."

Not necessarily, Geoffrey thought, following Enoch out into the pale light of morning. He paused and stretched, breathing in the smell of dry hay, warm manure, and soft dirt. Soon the sun would heat the side of the old gray barn, but now the walk to the house was shaded and cool. Behind him, he could hear the grooms and stable boys hurrying to let the animals out of the stalls. He could hear the creak of hinges and the answering whickers of welcome. The manor where his brother and mother lived seemed much farther away than the three miles of pasture.

"Are you happy here, Enoch?" he asked the man's retreating back.

Enoch stopped and turned to eye him. "Delirious," he snapped.

Geoffrey grinned. "Yes, I should have been able to tell. Sorry."

Enoch continued to eye him. "Are you?" he barked suddenly.

Geoffrey looked around at the barns, the green pastures rolling off on all sides, the horses starting off the day. "Oh, yes," he breathed. "Most of the time." Then somewhere in the distance it seemed to him that he heard the strains of waltz music. He glanced around again, and suddenly, everything looked empty. He had never felt so alone. His smile faded.

"Go home," Enoch ordered. "Go back to Wenwood. You won't be happy until that girl is your wife."

Geoffrey started. "Am I that transparent?"

"Clear as the brook in winter," Enoch replied. "Go home, Geoffrey. Go today."

Was it that easy? Geoffrey wondered, glancing about one last time. Could he simply go home and confess that he realized what was most important to him now? "Do you think Alan will let me?" he asked Enoch.

Enoch shrugged. "Why not? He sent you here for a purpose, didn't he? Have you accomplished it?"

Geoffrey started to laugh. "He sent me here to show me what will happen to me if I don't learn how to behave as a gentleman. You were supposed to be a bad example, Enoch. Only I find I rather admire you."

"Oh?" Enoch raised an eyebrow in challenge. "Why?"

"You're honest. You put your heart into the work you do; one only has to look at your horses to know that. You don't care for the villagers' regard, but you'd go out of your way to help them if they needed it. I daresay your conscience is clear."

"But I made you work, lad, harder I'll wager than you've ever worked before. And as you said, your reward was a filling meal and a bed of straw with the other lads."

Geoffrey shrugged. "So, I didn't get to be the pampered second son of the biggest landowner in these parts. What you had me doing was a lot more interesting than tagging about after Dutch Mattison or Tom Harvey, which is what I would have been doing. I actually learned more than I thought possible—about horses, and about standing on my own. I rather liked being simply Geoffrey Pentercast and getting along on my own wits for a change."

"What makes you think that isn't exactly what your brother intended you to learn?"

Geoffrey stared at him, his grin slowly spreading.

Enoch clapped him on the shoulder. "Go home, Geoffrey."

By lunchtime, Geoffrey had done just that. His mother was delighted to see him, Alan gave him a brotherly hug, and Genevieve leaned over a swelling belly to kiss him on the cheek. He had expected them to be just as angry with him as when he had left, but everyone was welcoming and pleasant. He went to great pains to behave properly, but no one seemed to notice how much he had changed. He was bemused by his entire reception. But that didn't stop him from taking Alan out for a ride later that afternoon. Riding was definitely safer than sitting about trying to converse with his mother and Genevieve, although he did don the navy tailored coat and chamois trousers his sister-in-law had purchased him for his birthday last spring. He needn't have bothered; Alan wore his usual tweed coat and trousers and looked every bit the country squire as they set off across the fields and through the woods of the estate.

"I must say, sending you to Enoch worked out rather well," Alan told him when they stopped atop the knoll overlooking the Munroe and Pentercast estates. The Abbey perched below them, and over the treetops they could see the barns and fields of the manor, stretching to the curve of the river Wen and beyond. Geoffrey had always liked the view from the top, although he would have preferred to have had another riding companion. He heard his brother's comment as if from a distance and decided it was better to laugh than be annoyed. "I suppose you have a right to crow. I do have a different perspective on life now. I know what I want. It has never been clearer to me."

"Oh?" He had obviously piqued his brother's interest. "And what would that be?"

Geoffrey pointed to the lush pasture on the other side of the river Wen. "That land, for starters. There must be at least thirty acres of good bottomland."

Alan raised an eyebrow. "So, you want to farm?"

"No," Geoffrey grinned. "I want to raise horses." When Alan failed to catch his enthusiasm, he hurried on. "Don't you see, Alan, it's the one thing we've never mastered? You've got a fine herd of dairy cows, even after the flood last winter, and a good size flock of sheep. The orchard and fields produce nicely. What are you missing for a truly great farm?"

"Pigs?" Alan suggested.

Geoffrey scowled at him. "There is no glory in being a pig farmer. No, Alan, we need horses, sturdy percherons for farming. That chestnut I saw in your back pasture is nearly past its last prayers, and I'm not much more pleased with the others I saw in the stables. How did you get any work done this season?"

Alan looked amused. "As I said, you've obviously learned a great deal. I can see I should have taken you with me when I purchased them."

Geoffrey shook his head. "I'll wager you paid too much for them, too. If you had your own stable, you wouldn't have to be at the mercy of horse thieves."

"Somehow I doubt the sellers at Wells would care for that appellation," Alan replied. "You're quite serious about this, aren't you?"

"I am. I want the Pentercast stable to be the finest in England."

"Lofty goal. What does Enoch think of this? He has the best stable going right now."

"True," Geoffrey acknowledged, "but he doesn't wish to raise the draft horses. I'll leave the riding horses to him." Geoffrey pointed to the land again, sketching his dream with his hand. "I'll put the house and barns there, on higher ground, where they won't be affected by the river's flooding."

"Very wise," Alan agreed, but Geoffrey got the impression from the smile on his brother's face that Alan was humoring him. Geoffrey ignored him.

"We'll have most of it in pasture and some for feed grain. I'm going to use the money Father left me to buy a pair of percherons, the strongest I can find. It will be a small start, Alan, but a start nonetheless." He turned to his brother, defensiveness rising despite himself. "Well, what do you say?"

Alan eyed the pasture for a moment more, then nodded. "It sounds like a marvelous plan. The land is yours. I'll have Carstairs draw up the papers."

Geoffrey threw back his head and crowed. "Fantastic! Alan, I cannot thank you enough. You won't regret it, I promise. This is going to make the Pentercast name famous."

"Better famous," Alan grinned, "than infamous."

Geoffrey grinned back. "Have no fear there. Now, there's only one thing left to arrange, and it is by far the more important."

"Oh?" Alan prompted again.

Geoffrey felt his grin deepen. "I have something to offer Allison at last. I was going to wait until she came home from London; but the way I'm feeling, I may just ride up there today. As I said, Alan, I finally know what's important to me. This stable is only a means to an end. What I want most in life is Allison Munroe for my wife."

Alan's face fell, and Geoffrey had a premonition of dread.

"What is it?" he demanded. "Has something happened to her? Why didn't you tell me?"

Alan shook his head. "She's quite well, old man. I'm very sorry, Geoffrey. I knew you were fond of Allison, but I never realized your feelings went beyond a mild flirtation." He moved his horse closer so he could put his hand on Geoffrey's shoulder. Geoffrey felt as if it were an anvil. "We received the news from Mrs. Munroe yesterday. Allison is engaged. She is to marry the Marquis DeGuis in November."

"No," Geoffrey said and felt a frustrated laugh of denial building inside him. "No, you're wrong. She wouldn't. She couldn't. Damn it, Alan, she's mine!"

Alan's look of pity only served to fuel his anger. With a wild yell, he whirled the horse and sent it galloping down the slope. It couldn't be true. He wouldn't let it be true! How much penance could one man bear? He had served his sentence, had even learned from it. Was he to be denied the blessing he craved beyond all things?

He took his case to the one court that might have some jurisdiction. Throwing the reins to a groom who came hurrying up at his sudden arrival at the Pentercast stables, he stalked into the house to find Genevieve.

"Tell me it isn't true," he demanded as he crossed the threshold into the withdrawing room, where his sister-in-law was taking a restorative sip of tea.

She reminded him rather frighteningly of her mother as she set the cup down on the teak table beside the chaise longue on which she rested, smoothed her sprigged-muslin skirts over her abdomen, and frowned. "I would probably be happy to, if you would explain to what we are referring."

"Allison and the Marquis DeGuis. She cannot have chosen to become engaged to him. This must be your mother's idea."

Genevieve smiled, obviously oblivious to his pain. "Oh, I wouldn't be so sure, Geoffrey. You have never met the marquis. I would say there are few young ladies who could resist his charms."

Geoffrey's heart sank, but he couldn't let his dream die so easily. "I don't believe it," he declared, flinging himself down on the rose-colored sofa across from her.

"One of your sister's foremost qualities is her loyalty. She promised to wait for me."

Genevieve's smile faded, and for a moment he wondered if she were going to scold him for dirtying the cheerful room with the dust from his boots. He was relieved when she chose to focus on the matter at hand instead. "Are you saying, Geoffrey, that you and my sister have an understanding?"

Much as he would have liked to tell her so, he knew it to be a lie. He had been too craven, even at the end, to hear the words that would have bound her to him. Leaving it in innuendo, he could not now claim she had made any promises. "No," he sighed. "Nothing so formal as that, worse luck. How could I ask her when I had nothing to offer?"

"And you do now?" Gen asked gently.

Before he could answer, Alan strode into the room. He looked clearly relieved to have found his brother. "Thirty acres of good bottomland," he declared as if he had been part of the conversation all along. "And the plans for a fine stable of farm horses, something much needed in this area. He has my support, love."

Genevieve's smile returned. "It certainly sounds as if you've been thinking through what you want to do, Geoffrey. Your plans would please Allison, I'm sure. You have my support as well. We have only two problems— Mother and the marquis."

"Do you truly think she loves him?" Geoffrey felt compelled to ask. "If he is as magnificent as everyone says . . ."

"Be assured he is," Genevieve replied, patting the seat of the nearby armchair to encourage Alan to sit beside her. "But Allison is loyal, as you said, and she is fond of you, Geoffrey, I know. Still, this will not be easy. You will have to show her that you are every inch the gentleman the marquis is."

"Allison won't need much convincing, I wager," Alan put in, seating himself and taking his wife's hand. "The person you will have to impress is Mrs. Munroe."

"Hang Mrs. Munroe," Geoffrey declared, buoyed by their support. "If Allison says the word, we're off to Gretna Green, and no one will stop us."

"No, Geoffrey," Gen said firmly even as his brother frowned. "Running away to Scotland to be married isn't the answer. Remember your own words—Allison's shining trait is her loyalty. Can you imagine what it would do to her to make her choose between her family and the man she loves?"

"She's right, Geoffrey," Alan agreed. "This dream of yours will die aborning if you divide the families again."

Geoffrey sighed, hemmed in on all sides. "You're right, of course. I just wish I had a better hope of reaching Mrs. Munroe."

"Leave Mother to me," Genevieve told him. "You concentrate on showing everyone how much you've changed." She paused, frowning at him. "You *have* changed, Geoffrey, haven't you? I don't think I'm up to ferrets in the kitchen."

"Or the ball room." Alan nodded.

Geoffrey glanced between the two of them. "I haven't changed the way I feel about Allison, unless you count how those feelings have deepened. But I think I can comport myself properly in polite society." He grinned. "And if I haven't changed, God have mercy on us all."

Nine

Allison slumped on the brown leather upholstery of the Munroe carriage across from her mother, watching the scenery recede behind them.

"Sit up, Allison," her mother murmured. Despite the jostling of the carriage, she carefully inserted the needle into the embroidery on her lap so that it did not touch the soft gray of her cloak. "You'll wrinkle your pelisse. A lady should never look unduly rumpled after traveling."

Allison glanced down at her own blue pelisse. Part of her wanted nothing more than to rend the thing from end to end if it would serve to ruffle her mother's implacable will, but it was a lovely sky blue with darker blue embroidery along the hem, collar, and cuffs, and the broadcloth was soft and comfortable. It seemed a shame to ruin it simply to spite her mother. Reluctantly, she straightened. Then, seeing the satisfied smile on her mother's lips, she slumped into an even smaller ball. Her mother sighed and continued pulling the needle along its course.

She was being ridiculous, she knew. Her sullen behavior only served to reinforce her mother's dismal opinion of her maturity, but she couldn't seem to stop herself. She had been so good—she had been pleasant, quiet, and ladylike all Season, hoping it would earn her the right to make her own choices; and now the most important choice she could make was being made for her. She had tried pleading, arguing, and crying. Nothing she had said or done had dissuaded her mother that she would not marry the marquis. It was maddening!

She would, of course, ultimately refuse. She was not in love with the marquis; it would be dishonest to marry him, not to mention that it would prevent her from marrying someone she did love. But announcing it so blandly would shame her mother, and despite her anger, she wasn't willing to do that.

She had even gone so far as to attempt to explain her feelings to the man himself when he had called a few days before they were to leave for the country. She felt she owed him that much. Once she had gotten over her initial shock of her mother's announcement, she had realized what an honor the marquis had done her. Out of dozens of lovely, accomplished, well-bred young ladies, he had chosen her for his marchioness. She could not deny that Lady Allison, Marchioness DeGuis, had a nice sound. But when she considered the staid, proper, utterly joyless lifestyle that seemed to go with it, the words rang hollow.

She did not wish to offend him. Surely if he had offered for her, he must feel more than he showed. However, she could not convince herself that he actually loved her. She had a difficult time imagining the marquis passionate about anything. Still, she must find a way to refuse him gently.

Her mother, of course, had not been willing to allow them any time alone. Perhaps it was her usual respect for propriety, but Allison suspected her mother knew what her daughter intended. She tried not to let that deter her as Perkins announced the marquis.

He bowed over her mother's hand first, then hers. But as he held her hand no longer or more firmly than her mother's, she was given no clue as to his feelings.

His smile as he sat across from her in his navy morning coat was no warmer or more personal than usual, his blue eyes above the pristine cravat as calm and candid as always. Allison sighed. It was not going to be easy to tell the man nearly every debutante wanted to marry that the one debutante he wanted did not want him.

"I trust your sister and the squire are well," he ventured.

Allison settled back in the chair, patting down the skirts of her sprigged-muslin gown, used to the routine by now. She felt her mother watching her from the sofa and tried not to show she noticed. "They are both well, thank you. You will see for yourself shortly, I understand."

"Yes." He smiled at her mother. "Your mother was kind enough to invite me to join you in the country."

"We are delighted you chose to accept," her mother replied with firmness that dared Allison to contradict her.

He inclined his head in acknowledgment.

"I understand something else as well," Allison forced herself to continue. "Mother tells me you have done me the honor of asking for my hand in marriage."

Something flickered behind the clear blue eyes, but it was gone before she could identify what. "I'm glad we no longer need to dissemble in that regard," he replied calmly. "I would much rather be your fiancé than merely another of your suitors."

She could imagine how much he disliked being part of the pack. "I own that it was a bit of a surprise."

He smiled at her, but the smile seemed to Allison to be that of a fond uncle and not an impassioned lover. "It was a bit of a surprise to me as well. I did not expect to meet someone like you."

Allison bit her lip. That could be his most lover-like statement so far or it could be a polite way of saying she was an impressive oddity. She could see the faintest of frowns on her mother's face and knew she was treading the line on impropriety.

"Nor did I expect someone like you to show interest," Allison hurried on before her mother could stop her. "We are so different, my lord. Do you not fear that we will not suit?"

He leaned forward, and suddenly the blue of his eyes seemed to block out every other sight in the room. "I think, Miss Munroe, that we will suit admirably. You are exactly the kind of woman I've always dreamed of marrying."

"And you are exactly the kind of man I dreamed of marrying," Allison cried. "Until last Christmas."

He frowned, glancing between her and her mother, and the world opened up again. "Last Christmas?"

"She is referring to her sister's courtship," her mother assured him. "It has nothing to do with the current circumstances." As before, her tone dared Allison to disagree.

"I was referring to our last sojourn at the Abbey," Allison compromised. She found it difficult to bring Geoffrey's name into the conversation with both the marquis and her mother frowning at her. "There is something about the country that helps one put things in perspective. Before then, I was looking only to marry the most presentable bachelor of the *ton*. However, last Christmas made me realize there is more to a husband than his position in Society or the cut of his coat."

The marquis looked thoughtful. "And may I ask what those qualities might be?"

Allison could not help but look at him in exasperation. Of all the times, why did he have to choose now to wish to converse on a subject of depth? But he had offered her an opening and she would be stupid not to take it.

"A kind heart," she started. "Loyalty to one's family and friends, a joy of the simple things in life such as the sunrise, a good harvest, a child's smile."

"Interesting," the marquis mused. "Those are the very traits I find appealing in you."

"Really?" Her amazement was out before she could think better of it.

"Really," he smiled, then he sobered. "I'm not sure London has given us a chance to get to know each other, Miss Munroe. I like to think I have other qualities besides the cut of my coat and my title. I hope you will allow me some time in the country."

She would have been the rudest creature alive to tell him no. She glanced at her mother, but the widow Munroe was gazing out the window in placid contemplation. She had the distinct feeling she was being manipulated; but again, she found it difficult to turn down so presentable a gentleman simply because her mother had been arrogant enough to accept his suit for her daughter. Allison sighed. "Very well. But I want it understood that the choice is mine. My mother may have accepted your suit, but I am the one who will decide whether we marry."

Her mother's eyes were snapping fire. Allison knew only the presence of the marquis was keeping her from getting the scold of her life. She raised her chin and glared back.

The marquis did not seem to notice their hostility. "Of course, Miss Munroe. You must forgive me for being old-fashioned. My own parents had an arranged marriage, and I will shortly have to arrange a marriage for my younger sister Catherine since our parents have now passed on. I regret that you have not been able to meet her yet. She is quite devoted to an elderly aunt of ours and has not been willing to leave her all Season. I hope to prevail upon her to return in November before our wedding, should you agree to marry me. Again, I apologize for not coming to you sooner. I should have realized a young lady like you would want to be included in the discussion. We will make no further arrangements without your participation, I promise."

Allison couldn't help beaming at him in approval, then turning to smile in triumph at her mother. The widow Munroe managed a grimace that resembled the look one had with a sore tooth rather than pleasure at his gesture. "How gracious, my lord," she murmured.

"Anything to show Miss Munroe how serious I am about my suit," he replied, rising. "And now, I have kept you, too long. Mrs. Munroe, Miss Munroe, always your servant." He bowed to them both. "I look forward to our time in the country."

If only she could look forward to it, she thought as they skirted the edge of the Mendip Hills, putting the bustle of Wells behind them. Each mile they drove grew more familiar; each mile made London seem farther away and longer ago. Soon she would be seeing her sister, Chimes and Annie at the Abbey, the fields and forests of her home. Soon she would have her talk with Alan and make him let Geoffrey out of his prison. She would have enjoyed her return fully if it hadn't been for the carriages behind them, bringing a piece of London with her.

She was restive enough, apparently, that her mother declared her companionship distracting. When they made the last pause to rest the horses at a coaching inn outside Wells, the widow Munroe insisted on changing places with Bryce in the second carriage. While Allison didn't mind a few moments without her mother's watchful company, certainly Bryce's company was not much better. She felt as if she had merely exchanged an eagle for a hawk.

"What does she think I'll do?" Allison complained

with ill humor as the little, dark-haired maid climbed into the coach. "Take Pippin and convince John Coachman to gallop off to Cornwall without her?"

"Whyever would you want to go there?" Bryce frowned. "The Abbey is in Somerset."

Allison shook her head. "Never mind, Bryce." She turned to gaze out the windows as the abigail settled herself and they started off once more.

They rode in silence for a while, Bryce mending a lace collar for the widow. Allison sighed, staring moodily out the window. Why did she have the feeling that her mother was going to make this visit even more unpleasant than their time in London? She tried to remember what it had been like when Gen was having her Season. Had her mother been this managing even then? Then the answer came back to her. Of course she hadn't been this managing; Rutherford Munroe had been alive. Her father had had a unique ability to get her mother to see reason. He was the only person she knew who had been able to get her mother to truly smile. For the first time in a long time, she wished he was with her still.

The vista before her was unpeopled, enhancing her feeling of being alone in the world. Outside, the wine rows gave way to fields of grain rippling to the rise of the hills. Only an occasional hedgerow blocked her view. As they passed one, the hills nearer Wenwood opened up. Atop the nearest, silhouetted against the midday sun, sat a lone horseman. Allison blinked, sitting a little straighter.

Bryce must have caught her movement, for she began to gather up her work. "Are we nearly at the Abbey, Miss Allison?" she asked.

Allison shook her head. "We still have a few miles to go. But someone is watching our procession."

Bryce peered out the window, then paled. "A highwayman!"

Allison laughed. "Surely not. Probably some farmer inspecting his fields. We make a lovely show for him, do we not?"

As if to refute her assertion, the horse reared, hooves pawing the air, the rider leaning forward to remain in the saddle. Then horse and rider plunged down the hillside, straight for the road.

"Lord have mercy!" Bryce cried.

Allison beamed at the wide-eyed abigail. "Come closer to the window, Bryce, so you can get a better view. It appears as if we are to be entertained before we even reach the Abbey."

Bryce swallowed and looked anything but entertained. Allison only grinned and returned her gaze to the window. This was her idea of excitement. Bryce was pale, and she wagered that if the widow Munroe were looking, she would be frowning. She wondered if it were a highwayman, would the marquis in the third carriage come forward with a pistol to defend them? The only person who might enjoy such a spectacle more was Geoffrey Pentercast.

As the rider closed the distance, she could see he rode a magnificent roan stallion, nearly as big and fast as the legendary Samson, Enoch McCreedy's prize breeder. Goooseflesh pimpled her arms suddenly, and she caught her breath. Try as she might, she could not make out a face at this distance and the rider wore a top hat in danger of falling off with his pounding ride so that she could not tell the color of the hair. Still, the shoulders were broad enough and the frame powerful enough to be Geoffrey. She craned forward.

"I don't much like this," Bryce muttered as the rider swept nearer and Allison strained to see him better. "I'm going to tell the coachman to stop." She started to rise to rap on the panel above them. Allison grabbed her and pulled her back into her seat.

"You will do nothing of the kind. The coachman has a better view than we do. If he thinks we're in danger, he'll do something about it." Indeed, it seemed to her as if the coach had picked up speed. Perhaps their driver sought to outrun the swiftly approaching horseman. As if he knew it, too, the rider bent low over the horse's neck, urging him on. Moments later, they burst out of the grain, flying toward the low hedgerow that separated the road from the fields.

"Is he mad?" Bryce gasped. "He'll never clear the hedge and the ditch!"

"And we won't be able to see in another minute!" Allison grabbed the window and forced it down even as Bryce cried out in protest. The wind swirled through the opening, whipping their hair about their faces. Allison clambered up on the seat and stuck her head out of the window.

"Oh, come in, Miss Allison, do," Bryce pleaded. Then even she seemed to catch the excitement. "Can you see him? Has he jumped? Did he make it?"

"He's nearly there," Allison reported, heart in her throat. Ahead, the row loomed larger than she had remembered. Even on Samson, he was a fool to try it. But what a magnificent fool!

Across from her, Bryce muttered a prayer.

The stallion's speed never slackened. The rider never hesitated. Even his top hat stayed miraculously on his head. The horse plunged toward the hedge, bunched his hind quarters, and sailed through the air to land on the verge of road and dash across the pebbled path.

Allison nearly collided with Bryce in her hurry to get to the opposite side of the carriage. Even as she pressed her nose to the glass, she felt the equipage slowing and heard a hail from ahead. The pounding hooves stilled, but in the quiet her heart seemed to pound even more loudly. Ahead, the rider had managed to turn and slow his mount. Even now, they drew abreast. Allison bit her lip, afraid to hope.

The rider came into view, a dusty if impeccably dressed Corinthian with a red riding habit boasting black velvet lapels, black trousers, and tasseled Hessians. Geoffrey would never have dressed so fashionably, even to impress someone he was courting. Allison's heart sank.

The carriage rocked to a stop. She could barely stand to look at the fellow, so keen was her disappointment that it was not Geoffrey. Bryce glanced at her, then lowered the carriage window herself.

"Good afternoon, ladies," the apparition spoke in a deep voice like a caress. Allison's head came up, and she stared in amazement at the laughter in those familiar brown eyes.

"Welcome to Wenwood." Geoffrey Pentercast grinned at them, touching the brim of his top hat and sketching a bow from the saddle. "I thought I'd ride out to greet you."

Ten

His grin widened as the smile spread on Allison's face, lighting her eyes. The sun echoed in her curls, tousled as if she, too, had just raced the wind. His humor was only helped that at her side, instead of a devoted fiancé, sat a wide-eyed Bryce.

Allison put her gloves together and applauded. "Well done, Geoffrey! Your time with Enoch McCreedy has definitely been well spent."

His smiled turned rueful and he couldn't help glancing down at his attire. "It was your sister told me to dress like this."

Allison laughed, the sound as welcome as the cool water of the brook that threaded its way through the Munroe/Pentercast woods. "I was not referring to your clothes, Geoffrey, but the fact that you're riding Samson. I do not recall anyone in Wenwood being accorded the honor before."

"Enoch knew this was important to me," he replied, rather hoping she would understand and that the others might not. To his dismay, she paled. However, before he could ask what troubled her, he was hailed from farther along the caravan. Allison turned with Bryce at the sound. She saw who approached from the second carriage and rolled her eyes.

Geoffrey eyed Perkins, telling himself this was only the first of the trials before him. The man walked slowly and regally to the first carriage, nose slightly lifted. It might have been the dust that he was trying not to inhale, but Geoffrey rather thought it was a comment on the present company. The man ignored Allison and Bryce, then paused to gaze up at Geoffrey from a position just below Samson's flared nostrils. His gaze was without the usual rancor, which surprised Geoffrey.

"Pardon me, sir," he intoned, "but Mrs. Munroe would like to know why our journey is delayed. She does not believe we have made your acquaintance."

Geoffrey's grin flashed. He was doing better than he had expected if even Perkins failed to recognize him. "You cannot know how delighted I am to hear that, Perkins. Please convey my apologies to Mrs. Munroe and assure her we have been introduced many times. It was not my intent to delay you, but to escort you. The roads can be difficult for a group of such lovely ladies traveling alone. As a local landowner, I thought to provide assistance. Of course, had I known they were already escorted by a gentleman of your caliber, I need not have bothered."

Perkins allowed himself the smallest of satisfied smiles. "I shall be happy to relay the information, sir. Will you ride with us to the Abbey, then?"

"With Miss Munroe's gracious permission." Geoffrey nodded a bow toward Allison, forcing Perkins to turn and acknowledge her existence. He didn't seem too pleased that the choice was hers. Allison's smile was just as satisfied as his had been moments before.

"Permission graciously granted," she sang out. Perkins turned to bow to Geoffrey. "Your servant, sir." As he walked back to the other carriage, Geoffrey turned with no little satisfaction to find Allison frowning at him.

"Coming on a bit strongly, aren't you?" she asked, wondering at how smoothly he had handled the butler when only months before she would have had to hold him to keep him from striking the man. "Or has your time with Enoch truly changed you, after all?"

He wanted to blurt out exactly how it had changed him; but now was neither the time nor the place, not with Bryce frowning in the background. Besides, Allison almost made it sound as if she thought the change was not for the better. "I suppose only time will tell," he hedged.

Beneath him, Samson stamped his feet restlessly, and he realized the other horses fretted in their traces. He swung Samson around. The coachman obviously took the cue, clucking to his own team, and the cavalcade set off once more.

Geoffrey would have liked to continue the conversation with Allison, but the rattle and creak of carriage and harness made it impossible. He tried to at least offer her a grin, but the women had been forced to close the windows to keep out the dust, and all he could see was his own uneven reflection. Frustrated, he gave Samson his heel and rode up ahead of the coaches to the Abbey.

Inside the carriage, Allison sat across from Bryce, a matching frown on her face.

"So," Bryce murmured, obviously perplexed. "That was Master Geoffrey?"

"No," Allison replied, shaking her head. "That was a changeling, Bryce, someone the fairies put in Geoffrey Pentercast's place. You've heard the stories about Enoch McCreedy. Would it surprise you that he practiced witchcraft?"

Bryce paled again, eyes so wide that Allison wondered whether the poor girl was having apoplexy.

"It was a joke, Bryce!" she cried.

Bryce swallowed. "A very poor one, Miss Allison. So, who was that?"

"As he said," Allison replied, turning away in hopes she might discourage conversation so she could think, "only time will tell."

Geoffrey outdistanced them to the Abbey by an easy five minutes. Of the two houses on what had once been the Munroe estate, he vastly preferred his own manor to the Abbey. Low-slung and sprawling, the house crouched amidst the woods of Wenwood, a small clearing at its front and a pond and gardens at its back. Many of its front windows were no more than slits; Allison's father had at least had the sense to replace some of the rear-facing windows with wider panes so that many of the common rooms had light and air. Still, he found it a brooding place. He hadn't been up here since Allison had left.

At the sound of his arrival, grooms hurried from the stables to the left of the house and the darkly paneled double front doors swung wide, spilling footmen into the clearing. Behind them limped an older man, his white hair sparse about his ears, but the devilment in his nearly black eyes still evident.

"Hello, Chimes," Geoffrey heralded, pulling Samson to a stop.

"Hello yourself, you young jackanapes," Chimes grumbled. "Stand down, men. We thought you were someone."

Geoffrey laughed. "I am someone, Chimes. You should know that. However, the important ones are hard on my heels. If you listen, you'll hear the sound of their passing."

Chimes frowned but paused, cocking his head and lifting his long nose so that he resembled nothing so much as Alan's favorite pointer. A low rumble built in the distance. He nodded. "Right you are, Mr. Geoffrey. Thanks for the warning."

Geoffrey grinned at him "Thought you might want time to get into your coat, even if you haven't worn it since they left."

Chimes grinned back, showing the gap between his two front teeth. "I misplaced it months ago. Besides, I wouldn't put it on even if I could find it. Her nibs will get used to me again, I warrant."

Geoffrey had another of his premonitions of dread. So, Chimes didn't know about Perkins. If Geoffrey was any judge, their meeting would be worse than the Battle of Vitoria. Down the drive, the rumble grew louder, and the cavalcade began pulling into the clearing. The footmen hurried forward to assist the arrivals; the grooms dashed up to settle the horses. Samson whickered his disapproval at being still so long. Geoffrey absently patted his neck, watching as Allison alighted.

She had changed. He could see it when she moved. Her carriage was taller, more elegant than he had remembered, her movements graceful and sure. The hug she gave Chimes seemed restrained. When she whispered something in his ear, he frowned. *Ah,* Geoffrey thought, *intelligence about the other side.* She straightened, offering a supportive smile. Then she glanced up to meet his eye and everything seemed to stop for a moment.

He has changed, Allison thought, gazing at Geoffrey across the bustle and noise of the clearing. He sat straighter on Samson, even in the clothes that didn't seem to be his, sure of who he was and what he wanted. By the look on his face, she knew that what he wanted was her. The knowledge frightened her down to her soul. She turned from him, closing her eyes and taking a deep breath. When she had taken herself in hand and had the courage to look back, he had dismounted and was leading Samson around the back of the house.

Geoffrey had watched an answering fire spring to Allison's eyes before she turned away. He caught his breath, but before he could think of an appropriate response, the next carriage trundled into the yard, followed shortly by the third. The clearing was filled with horses and people, bags and baggage, shouts and calls. He dismounted Samson and led him around back before the horse could grow more restless.

Tying him with a lead to the branch of a tree, Geoffrey hurried back in time to see a tall, dark-haired man alight from the third carriage. He was well-favored, broad shouldered, and lean legged. His impeccable, well-tailored clothes and easy grace marked him as a peer of the realm. It didn't take much to deduce that this was the Marquis DeGuis. Geoffrey grit his teeth. He hadn't expected her to bring the man with her. What was he, some trained lapdog?

From his vantage point, Geoffrey watched the marquis saunter through the chaos as if he strolled through Hyde Park on a day with little crowd. Behind him scurried a valet carrying a gentlemen's toiletry box of polished inlaid wood. The valet, his coachman, and his grooms moved with efficiency and purpose no lapdog could have inspired. Geoffrey's eyes narrowed.

The marquis joined the group near the front door, making a bow to the ladies in general. Geoffrey watched Allison, feeling as if he could hardly breathe. But Allison merely nodded politely and returned to her conversation with her mother. No lover-like reunion this. She'd been more welcoming to him when he had ridden to meet them.

Geoffrey sucked in a breath of the dust-filled, sweat-tanged air. Nothing had ever smelled sweeter. He had a chance after all. Allison was obviously not in love with

the marquis, at least not yet. Perhaps that was why the
man had followed her to the wilds of Somerset: he
needed time to consolidate his advantage. Geoffrey determined at that moment that he wasn't going to give
the man so much as a minute, if he could help it. He
strode forward with purpose.

In the clearing, Perkins was attempting to direct the
staff about their duties. The grooms who had remained
in Wenwood frowned at him, but kept about their business. Unfortunately, the work was obviously not going
to his liking, for as Geoffrey approached, he glanced
about and spied Chimes near the door.

"You there, fellow," he called. "See to Mrs. Munroe's
baggage."

Chimes straightened, black eyes crackling with light-
ning.

First salvo, Geoffrey thought. He hurried toward the
group by the door before the battle started in earnest.

Allison heard the call as well. She laid a hand on
Chimes's stiff arm. "That's him," she whispered. "Now,
mind your manners. Remember what I told you. Just
show him, and Mother, that you know how to run the
Abbey."

A muscle was working under Chimes left eye as he
squinted at the tall, imposing butler. "Seems to me no
one's had call to question that before."

"A lot of things have changed since Father died,"
Allison replied, giving his arm a squeeze. "We have all
had to learn new tricks."

She thought she was only trying to help him, but
something in her tone must have betrayed her recent
frustrations, for the sharp-eyed man-of-all-work turned
his gaze on her thoughtfully. "Miss Allison," he began.

"Ho, fellow," Perkins called impatiently, obviously un-
used to being ignored. "You are needed over here."

Chimes whipped to face him. "I'm needed a great many places," he proclaimed, striding forward.

Geoffrey slid into his place beside Allison. "Here comes the return fire," he quipped.

Allison caught his meaning immediately. "I'd rather this wasn't a war, if you please. Chimes has too much to lose."

"Is something wrong, Miss Munroe?" the marquis asked, eyeing Geoffrey.

Geoffrey was tempted to glare the man into submission, but he realized that would be acting tremendously like the Geoffrey Pentercast he was supposed to have left behind. Instead, he smiled and bowed.

"I don't believe we've met, my lord," he said. "I'm Geoffrey Pentercast. I believe you know my older brother, the squire."

The marquis's brow cleared, and he offered his hand. "Yes, of course, you would be the brother of Miss Munroe's sister's husband. I met your brother in London. I take it you're the local landowner who rode out to meet us."

"Yes, I am," Geoffrey replied congenially, trying not to like the man's cordial manner. He rather hoped it was all an act, but too many people had praised the man in his hearing for him to be sure. "I wanted to welcome you all to Wenwood." He turned back to Allison, who had that suspicious look on her face again. "Especially Miss Munroe, straight from her triumphant Season."

Allison managed a smile. She couldn't imagine what had gotten into him, fawning and smiling like an idiot. She half expected him to offer to shine the man's boots with his coat sleeve! "I used to so enjoy Mr. Pentercast's company," she replied airily.

Geoffrey tried not to wince at the past tense. He was sure he was being exactly the kind of man everyone had told him he was supposed to be. Yet it was only serving to set Allison's teeth on edge. He tried again.

"Will you be staying with us long?" he asked the marquis in what he hoped was a conversational tone.

"For a while," the marquis replied, offering Allison a smile. "The exact amount of time is up to Miss Munroe. My original plan was to stay until Guy Fawkes Day."

So long as that? Geoffrey grit his teeth and smothered a snarl of frustration. Then he brightened, realizing that once Allison agreed to cry off, the man would be packing in no time.

"That man is impossible," Mrs. Munroe declared, joining them. "My lord, I want to assure you that only Perkins will be serving you while you grace us with your presence."

"Perkins?" the marquis asked with a raised eyebrow.

Allison hid a smile at how unmemorable the snooty butler apparently was. She caught Geoffrey's eye, and he winked at her. The day seemed suddenly brighter, and she grinned back.

"Yes, Perkins, our London butler," Mrs. Munroe replied. She turned to the clearing and shaded her eyes from the late-afternoon sun. Allison followed her gaze, but the tall butler was nowhere in sight. Her mother frowned.

Chimes scampered up to the front doors and pushed them even farther open. "Sorry to take so long, my lord, ladies. This way, if you please."

Mrs. Munroe actually went so far as to scowl. Chimes swallowed. Geoffrey turned to Allison, only to find that the marquis had already offered his arm. She accepted it and allowed him to lead her in. Mrs. Munroe eyed him. Geoffrey considered the situation for ten seconds, then swept her a bow. "Mrs. Munroe, your servant." He offered her his arm. Her eyes narrowed, but she accepted it. He hoped it wasn't shaking as he led her in.

"Thank you," she murmured as he came to a stop in the wide parquet-floored entryway not far from Allison and the marquis. "You're very kind, Mr. . . ."

Geoffrey hid a grin of triumph. "You're welcome, dear lady. It is a pleasure to have you home with us again."

"Thank you," she repeated, studying him. He thought for a moment she had realized who he was, but then her brow knit in confusion again. He turned to Allison and the marquis.

"I will leave you to get settled, my lord, Miss Munroe. But before I go, allow me to extend an invitation from my mother. She would like it if you all could join her at a dinner in the marquis's honor two nights hence."

"I would be delighted," the marquis assured him. "With my hostess's permission, of course."

Mrs. Munroe nodded blankly. "Certainly." She raised narrowed eyes to Geoffrey's face. "Please tell your mother that we would be delighted to accept. And the dinner will be held at your estate, I assume?"

Geoffrey bowed. He glanced over at Allison to find her grinning at him again. His heart sang. "Yes, Mrs. Munroe. Dinner will be served at the manor at eight o'clock, if that is convenient for you."

Mrs. Munroe paled. "The manor?" She peered at him again and her pallor deepened. "Yes, of course, the manor. We shall see you then . . . Mr. Pentercast."

Eleven

By the third day after they had returned to the Abbey, Allison decided that she was the only person in the entire world who had not gone mad. Either that, or she had gone mad and was hallucinating the entire affair. There simply were no other explanations for the state of things.

No one was acting as she would have expected, with the possible exception of her mother. If Allison had been surprised by the change in Geoffrey when he had greeted them the first day, his behavior at the dinner party was even more uncharacteristic. Instead of insisting on walking beside her to dinner, he had offered his arm to her sister of all people, leaving a bemused Alan to escort her mother. As the senior person, the marquis had escorted the hostess, as was proper, leaving Allison to walk alone at the tail of the line.

At the dinner table, Geoffrey never belched once, though Allison kept looking at him, wondering if perhaps he might explode from the effort. He ate sparingly of each of the sumptuous dishes their cook had prepared and made pleasant conversation with Genevieve, who sat on his right. Allison, who sat across from him, wanted nothing so much as to kick him under the table to get his attention. Unfortunately, the large damask-draped table was much too wide for her to do more than to swing her foot through the air.

After dinner the three men lingered over their port
for so long that Mrs. Pentercast fell asleep waiting, her
tiny head bobbing to her ample breast like an overfed
robin. Mrs. Munroe and Genevieve chatted about nurs-
eries and feedings and layettes until Allison wanted to
scream in vexation. When the men did arrive, they were
so nauseatingly chummy that she could only tap her
foot and purse her lips. Neither Geoffrey nor the marquis had seemed to notice. The widow Munroe had
been so impressed by Geoffrey's behavior that she had
magnanimously invited him to partake of any of the
other events they might plan while the marquis was in
attendance.

As for the marquis, his behavior also bore little re-
semblance to what she had expected of him. He rose
each morning and rode the Arabian gelding he had
brought with him, a dainty dun-colored creature with
fire in his eyes and magnificent lines. He spent his
mornings hunting with Alan and sometimes Geoffrey
and his afternoons reading or catching up on corre-
spondence with his man of affairs or the stewards of his
many estates. If Allison deigned to join him on any of
his pursuits, he seemed quite glad for her company, but
he did not seek her out or in any way force his attentions on her. In fact, he was so far from the importunate
lover that Allison wondered whether she had dreamed
her mother's announcement of their engagement.

Chimes was acting nearly as civilized as the marquis,
mincing about in the only coat he owned, even though
his belly had outgrown it some time since, and attempting to take over every task assigned to Perkins. Perkins
had at first reacted with typical high dudgeon, long nose
in the air and back ramrod straight. However, of late,
Allison noticed he had been letting Chimes do most of
the work, stepping aside when the little man bustled
forward. At first Allison thought perhaps the taller man

had some heart after all, but then she had realized that it was not so much charity that let him allow Chimes to do the work, but a pronounced lazy streak. Mrs. Munroe had tried repeatedly to tell Chimes that she wished Perkins to serve during their stay, but each time she did so, their cook Annie, Chimes's wife, showed her displeasure by turning her usual mouth-watering meals into pure paste. In the end, Mrs. Munroe gave up the fight, at least until the marquis went home. Then Allison shuddered to think what was to become of the elderly couple who had cared for the Abbey, and the Munroes, for so long.

Her sister was perhaps the most changed of all. The last time Allison had seen her, Genevieve had been glowing with the news of her first child. Other than her beaming face, no one would have known she was expecting. Now, at seven months along, her sister was billowing out of any dress she attempted to wear. She still helped the dowager Mrs. Pentercast keep the manor, but her activities were more and more conducted from the chaise longue in the withdrawing room. It was there that Allison found her the morning of the day after they had arrived at the Abbey.

Genevieve hugged her close as Allison bent over the chaise, then patted the seat of the chair beside it for her to sit. "I'm so glad you're back!" her sister exclaimed, all smiles. "Tell me about the Season. I had your letters, of course, and Mother's, but it doesn't seem the same as talking to you."

Allison smiled back. "It was an interesting Season. You know how it is—balls, parties, the theater. Truth be told, it all seems a bit of a blur."

"And of your friends, how many collected proposals?"

Allison felt her smile fading. "Lady Janice collected any number of proposals, but she hasn't accepted a one. Poor Grace didn't so much as get a nod, unless you count the young man from York who nodded asleep in front of her. Cousin Margaret claims to be in love, but she refused even in the end to tell me who had stolen her heart. I certainly never saw any particular gentleman paying her court."

She could feel her sister studying her. "But I hear you are engaged."

"Not if I have anything to say about it." The words came out much too heatedly, and Allison sighed even as her sister frowned at her vehemence. "I'm sorry, Gen, but that is the way it is. Mother agreed to his proposal; I didn't even know about it until a few weeks ago."

"So, of course, you refused him."

"No." Allison had to stop herself from squirming under her sister's sharp-eyed gaze. "Honestly, Gen, he really is a dear. You cannot say I'll find someone more handsome or wealthier or more polished than the marquis."

The gaze didn't falter. "No, I certainly cannot say that. So, you have accepted him? I heard from Geoffrey that he came with you to the Abbey."

"Well," Allison huffed, feeling manipulated, "if you knew he was with us, why did you ask me whether I'd refused him? He'd hardly be here if I'd refused."

Genevieve studied her hands as they lay over her belly. "I'm sorry, Allison. I simply wanted to hear you say it in your own words. I certainly don't get the impression you are in love with him, for all that he is impressive."

Allison sighed. "Oh, I wish I knew! I should be in love with him, shouldn't I? Are we not agreed that he is the perfect candidate for my hand?"

"We are agreed that the marquis is a paragon," Genevieve corrected her. "I, for one, certainly never agreed that he was perfect for you. Only you can say that, Allison."

Allison sighed again. "I cannot say it, at least, not yet. I promised him some time in the country so that we might learn to know each other better."

Genevieve nodded, then caught her breath and put her hand to her stomach.

Allison leapt to her feet. "Is something wrong? Shall I go get Mrs. Pentercast or your abigail?"

"No," her sister replied with a shake of her head. She patted her belly and let her hand fall. "The baby just has a tendency to jump about at all the wrong moments. The other day when I was trying to inventory the upstairs linens, I thought perhaps my child had learned the gavotte. Perhaps we will finally have another to match your talent on the dance floor."

Allison smiled politely, but she felt a twinge of guilt. Genevieve should be spending her time preparing for the upcoming birth. She hardly needed to worry over Allison's problems of the heart. Allison resolved not to trouble her again.

But that left very few people for her to talk to as the days wore on. Her mother was preoccupied with baby matters, spending much time each day at the manor with Genevieve, Chimes was too busy pretending to be a butler, and she had never been able to talk to Alan or the marquis. She did try writing to Grace, her cousin Margaret, and Lady Janice, but she agreed with her sister that waiting for a reply was ever so much less satisfying than speaking face to face. That left only Geoffrey, and she found she missed their discussions most of all.

She had no idea what devious acts Enoch McCreedy had perpetrated to bring about the change in Geoffrey, but she could see their effects. It wasn't his smooth-tongued conversation that made her mother smile and the marquis nod appreciatively. The Pentercasts had long been known to be capable of calling on a ready wit. Even though she had seldom seen Geoffrey use it before now, she was not surprised to find that he possessed the talent as well. It certainly wasn't the dapper morning coats or patterned waistcoats he suddenly affected instead of his tweed coat and homespun trousers. His cravat was still nothing more than a knot at his neck, and she had yet to see him change his Hessians for evening pumps. No, she sensed something much more fundamentally different in his attitude, just as she had on the first day. He stood a little straighter, and he smiled more easily as if he suddenly understood his place in the world and found great contentment in that. And whenever he accompanied them, she felt his eyes on her. Each time she met his gaze it was thoughtful. He hadn't winked at her once.

She was afforded ample opportunities to see him, what with her mother's invitation that he join them in their outings and entertainments. It seemed to her that he visited nearly every day. He was always courteous and charming, but distant somehow, like a banked fire deep under a layer of cool ash. By the second week of their visit, she had determined that she was going to have a private word with him if she had to be outrageously rude to do it.

Her mother had suggested that she take the marquis on a walk around the Abbey grounds that morning. Allison had wondered if even her mother thought she needed to get the man alone to get him to show his more passionate side. She found herself considering the possibility that he had no passionate side. It was a crying waste of material, but entirely possible. Still, she was all the more pleased when Geoffrey, Gen, and Alan called just as they were about to set out.

Geoffrey bowed to Mrs. Munroe and Allison, nodding a good morning to the marquis. He had been playing the Society beau long enough that he knew the frustration that had been building for the last two weeks didn't show in his movements or expression. He had been the pattern card of gentlemanly virtue. His mother had remarked on it; Alan had remarked on it; Gen had praised it, and even Allison's mother had smiled at him. The only person who seemed displeased by his performance was the one person who mattered: Allison. He was determined that, today, he was going to get her alone and find out why.

"Going for a stroll?" Genevieve sighed at her mother's invitation to join the marquis and Allison. She laid her hand on her swollen belly and sighed again. "I'm afraid my days of strolling are nearing an end. Alan, why don't you join them? I have a few things to discuss with Mother."

Alan nodded wisely, and Geoffrey noticed the look they exchanged. He kept his smile to himself. Genevieve had been keeping her mother occupied for the better part of the two weeks. Today was the day she was going to bring up the engagement and his candidacy for Allison's hand. He stood a little straighter.

Allison noticed the look between her sister and brother-in-law as well. Now, what could they be up to? She was just as glad that Alan agreed to accompany them. It would give the marquis someone to talk to when she made off with Geoffrey.

They wandered through the rose gardens at the back of the house and reached the ornamental pond beyond. Hugging her blue pelisse to her in the early autumn sunlight, Allison pointed out her father's flock of swans, the functioning bell tower on the Abbey, the forest surrounding them.

"If you follow the path to the left," she pointed, "you will climb a rise with an excellent view of the surrounding land. I promised my mother that I'd check the weir at the end of the pond. We had some trouble with it last winter, if you recall, Mr. Pentercast."

Geoffrey blinked, as if he were surprised that she would single him out. Then his usual grin appeared, and she feared he would spoil everything. "Yes, of course, Miss Munroe. A dreadful flood, as I recall. You surely wouldn't want a reoccurrence."

"No, indeed," the marquis concurred. "Do you need assistance, Miss Munroe?"

Allison smiled brightly at him and ignored Geoffrey's scowl as she did so. "Thank you, but I hoped to prevail upon Mr. Pentercast, as he was aware of our difficulties and so should be able to spot any new problem."

"I'm sure Geoffrey will know just what to do," Alan put in with a conspiratorial grin. "He's had a great deal of experience studying farming recently."

Geoffrey bowed. "Your servant, Miss Munroe. Gentlemen, we will rejoin you shortly."

The marquis nodded, but Allison thought his eyes narrowed. She hurried Geoffrey away before her feeling of guilt could grow any larger.

They stood quite properly, at least four feet separating them, gazing down at the stone weir Alan had had installed to replace the wooden dam that had been destroyed on New Year's Eve. Geoffrey stomped his Hessian on the edifice.

"Solid as the Empire," he proclaimed. He looked up and caught her gaze on him. Allison felt the blood rush to her face at the warmth of his look.

"Are you all right?" he asked softly.

Allison swallowed. The last thing she had expected was concern for her. It left her pleased and unsure at the same time. "I wanted to ask you the same question. You've been acting rather strangely since we returned. Did Enoch McCreedy really do this to you?"

Geoffrey laughed. "My time with Enoch was enlightening, but I wouldn't say he is the reason for the change in me. You have more to do with that."

"Me?" Allison asked in astonishment. "Why on earth would you say that? I haven't even seen you in more than four months."

"But I see you, every day," he replied, leaning closer and watching her eyes widen, "in my dreams."

Allison took a deep breath. "I'm glad you think of me, Geoffrey," she told him truthfully. "I think of you often as well. Mostly, I miss you. Everyone around me is so stiff and proper! Can't we just have fun?"

His heart went out to her, but he knew he would never win her by just having fun. "As your sister likes to point out, we aren't children anymore, Allison. We all have to grow up."

Allison made a face. "Grow up and grow old and stuffy. Honestly, Geoffrey, isn't there more to life than witty conversation and a well-cooked dinner?"

"I certainly hope so," he declared. "Don't think I've gotten that sedate, my girl. But I've come to realize that it's time I settle down, settle down and get married."

He was watching her again. The look brought the color flooding back to her cheeks. She wondered suddenly if her sister had told him about her supposed engagement with the marquis. She had forgotten to ask, what with all the chaos around her. He had a right to know the truth about it. "I think Gen may have told you—" she started, the feelings of guilt returning. "That is, I think you know that—"

"That you're engaged to the marquis? Alan told me." He tried not to let her see the effort it cost him to say it coolly. "Is it what you want?"

"No!" she cried, surprised to find that she was still just as furious as when her mother had first announced the fact. "I didn't know, Geoffrey. You must believe me.

Mother agreed to the match without even consulting me."

"I knew it!" The words exploded out of him. His arms came up, and for a moment, she thought he would gather her to him. Then he stiffened, lowering his arms. "Then you've refused him?"

She hung her head. "I tried, in truth I did. But at the time it seemed to me that his feelings were engaged, if he has feelings in the same way we do. Since then I have begun to wonder again, but I dislike hurting him and it is an honor to be asked."

His voice was stilted, not at all like the Geoffrey she had known all her life. "Do you think you can grow fond of him?"

"Perhaps." Allison sighed. "But fondness is far too little of what I expected of my marriage. Shouldn't there be romance? Passion? Love?"

Again he looked on the verge of reaching for her, and again he stopped himself. She had never seen him so tense; his entire body was like an overwound spring in a clock. "If that is what you want in a marriage," he managed, "then you should wait until you have it."

She frowned. "But will it happen? Perhaps Mother is right and I am too young to realize that this fondness is all there is. Certainly I cannot say my mother loved my father in the way I thought I'd love my husband. Did your mother and father love that way?"

Geoffrey shrugged, the conversation more difficult than he had thought possible. "If they did, they never demonstrated it in my presence. But if you want an example, look at Alan and Genevieve. A more besotted pair you'll never see."

Allison felt as if a weight had been lifted. "Yes, of course! Thank you, Geoffrey. You are right—love *can* occur, even in these times. I suppose it remains to be seen whether it can occur between the marquis and me."

Geoffrey turned from her, eyeing the trees beside them, struggling to maintain his composure. "I am no expert in love, Allison. For some, I believe, love bursts into bloom suddenly, as it did for Genevieve and Alan last Christmas. For others, it seems to grow over time, strong and sure. I take it you have met no one who has made you feel as you wish?"

"No one." She sighed.

He flinched and turned back to her, his manner as withdrawn as the marquis's. "Pity. I suppose you will simply have to wait."

Even in the distance he had put between them, she could feel the tension still there, like a snake coiled beneath the unruffled surface of a pond. "Are you sure you're all right, Geoffrey?"

He laughed, but there was no joy in the sound. "Me? Why do you ask?"

"You seem—" She struggled to find the right word. "—angry? Disappointed? Frustrated with me? I just wanted you to understand that I remembered what you said before you left London."

"Did you?" he murmured.

"Yes, of course. You asked me to wait. And I did, only Mother didn't."

"That wasn't all I said."

She frowned, thinking back. The tension, his response to her thoughts, all suddenly made sense and she felt herself blushing again. "Oh, yes," she replied, unable to meet his gaze. "You said when I returned, you would stand your ground on your suit."

"My suit." The words sounded bitter. "Tell me, Allison, is that what you want? Another unloved suitor to deal with?"

She winced. "Not unloved, Geoffrey. I'm quite fond of you; you know that."

"And I think we just agreed that fondness is not the basis you want for marriage."

"I'm sorry." The sentiment sounded trite and the guilt she had shed moments ago returned, only stronger. She forced herself to straighten. "I'm sorry, Geoffrey," she repeated firmly. "I can't be something I'm not. You wouldn't want me to lie."

"Wouldn't I?" He snorted. Then he sighed. "No, I suppose I wouldn't. But I'll tell you one thing, moonling, it's my turn to wait. You see, my love for you has only grown stronger and surer. The question is, will I have the patience and courage to wait for yours to bloom?"

Twelve

Geoffrey needed both patience and courage over the next few weeks. He needed patience to continue showing Allison, Mrs. Munroe, and his family that he did indeed know how to behave like a gentleman. There were times when Mrs. Munroe said unthinking cruelties that brought tears to Allison's eyes and Geoffrey wanted nothing so much as to throttle her. On the other hand, there were times when Perkins was so plainly trying to ingratiate himself to Mrs. Munroe in order to gain Chimes's rightful place that he wanted to walk away in disgust. In both situations, he was forced to smile and turn aside any *faux pas* with a witty comment. Twice his attempts earned him a smile from Allison, and several times he caught the marquis eyeing him in silent approval. Surprisingly, both responses helped to ease his temper.

On the other hand, it took considerable courage to watch the marquis court Allison, even if it was in his own quiet style. Several times Geoffrey arrived for a morning call to find that they had already been out on a constitutional around the grounds together. Allison always seemed to look pleased and bubbly after such walks, her mood fading when she saw Geoffrey watching. Geoffrey had to watch silently while the marquis turned the pages of her music when she played to entertain their guests one night after dinner. He had to make conversation with the widow Munroe while the marquis held yarn for Allison while they all sat chatting by the fire one rainy day. He had to pretend to enjoy himself when the marquis read aloud from Shakespeare as they ate a picnic lunch on the knoll, his eyes lingering on Allison as he recited one love sonnet after another.

"He has every advantage," Geoffrey complained to Alan and Gen that night at the manor. "With the widow Munroe's penchant for quiet amusements, he is bound to come out better than I do."

"Allison must be bored beyond tears," Gen mused. "Quiet amusements are no more her cup of tea than yours."

Geoffrey stared at her for a moment, then sprang across the distance to give her a hug. "That's it!"

"What's it?" she asked, laughingly fending him off, obviously mindful of her growing belly.

Geoffrey grinned at her, hopeful for the first time in days. "Allison would be much happier with more lively amusements, and lively amusements are my specialty."

Genevieve eyed him. "And what about how you've changed?"

"In other words," Alan put in, "I sincerely hope there are no ferrets involved."

Geoffrey laughed. "No ferrets, but I cannot say the same for other animals." When both his brother and sister-in-law looked aghast, he could not help but laugh again. "Don't worry. I promise I will be a complete gentleman. I will simply work harder at finding a way to turn the situation to my advantage."

His chance came the very next day. He was to accompany Alan, Allison, and the marquis on an early morning ride around both estates. He had borrowed a snow-white gelding from Enoch the day before when he had gone up to fetch the bay foal to the manor. The gelding looked quiet and well-mannered, but Enoch had been unable to sell him because he had a regrettable tendency to want to race. Alan's horse was a slug, but he knew Allison's Blackie was always up for a run. He just wasn't sure about that dun Arabian gelding the marquis rode.

Allison eyed the white horse as Geoffrey and Alan rode up that morning. The snowy hide made Geoffrey's riding outfit look as red as blood and his hair as dark as night. While she thought Alan looked rather well in his green riding coat and the marquis was distinguished in black, Geoffrey seemed somehow more vibrant. Her spirits rose as she let the groom assist her into the side-saddle. She felt just as vibrant in her royal-blue velvet riding habit. She seized the end of the white silk scarf that held the jaunty top hat on her flaxen curls and tossed it over one shoulder. Geoffrey grinned at her, and the marquis smiled his approval. Surrounded by handsome, charming gentlemen, she set off.

They started off at a docile pace with Alan in the lead. Allison rode with the marquis on her right and Geoffrey on her left. She looked satisfied, but Geoffrey couldn't help wondering if she ever felt as if she were a bone being eyed by two dogs. He noticed the marquis watching him and quickly looked away.

They rode in quiet decorum down the way from the Abbey, pausing where it joined the main drive to the manor. Leaves were falling from the trees, speckling the lane with bright spots of gold and russet. Geoffrey eyed the drive thoughtfully, then winked conspiratorially at Allison, who brightened immediately.

"The last time we rode here, you beat me in a race to the manor," he accused her. "Are you game to try again?"

Allison returned his grin eagerly, and his heart soared.

"Always!" Then she glanced guiltily at the marquis. "Will you join us, my lord?"

The gentleman offered her a regretful smile, and Geoffrey hid a grin of triumph. "I think not, Miss Munroe. I want to see the track before I race my horses. I wouldn't want to risk Nicodemus here on faulty ground."

"Wise choice," Alan put in, frowning at Geoffrey, who ignored him.

Allison eyed the graceful gelding. "Yes, I suppose it is wise." Geoffrey watched as she obviously wrestled with the feasibility of leaving the marquis and Alan alone while she pelted off ahead. She sighed. "You are right. It has been months since I rode this way. Perhaps I'd better make sure it's safe as you suggest."

Geoffrey grit his teeth at how easily he had been thwarted, but he offered them a bow. "Very practical, to be sure." His mind whirled, trying to think of some way to get them back onto the subject. He brightened. "Perhaps if we determine the way to be decent, we can race on the way back."

Allison brightened as well, casting a look at the marquis out of the corner of her eye. "Would that suit you, my lord?"

Geoffrey wanted to shout at her for letting the man's whims dictate her actions, especially when she had claimed no allegiance to him, but he kept a polite smile on his face as the marquis's blue-eyed gaze swept his way. "Excellent suggestion, Pentercast. Let us proceed."

Allison settled back in the saddle, satisfied. Finally, they were to have some fun! The last few days had been suffocatingly staid. The marquis had been attentive, to be sure. In fact, most of the time she quite enjoyed his company. He had a way of making her smile that differed from anyone she had ever met. In the quiet of the country, she had finally gotten him to converse on something more personal than the weather, including his hopes to enclose the largest of his estates and his fondness for his younger sister, whom she found she was eager to meet. In fact, they were getting along better than she would have imagined, and all without the man raising so much as a finger to court her, in her opinion. But she had been longing to do something more active, and Geoffrey's suggestion of a race seemed to her to be perfect.

They rode on up the lane, Geoffrey working at hiding his impatience, until the road opened in front of the manor.

Alan shaded his eyes with his hand, gazing about with a frown.

"I don't see Genevieve on the porch as she promised. Perhaps I'd better check on her. Excuse me, gentlemen, Miss Allison. Don't let me stop you from your race."

Geoffrey grinned at him. "Don't worry, we won't." He turned to Allison and the marquis. "Well, my lord, was the track to your satisfaction?"

The marquis nodded, blue eyes gleaming brighter than Allison had ever seen. She looked at him in surprise, noting with approval the bright spots of color in his cheeks and the determined set of his mouth. She tightened the grip on her reins. This was going to be a race, after all.

"The road was quite good, Pentercast," the marquis told him. "I say, let's do it."

"Excellent!" Geoffrey crowed, not caring if he sounded too enthusiastic for a man-about-town. "Will you give the word, my lord?"

The marquis turned to Allison, touching his quirt to his top hat. "It appears we are off. See you at the Abbey, my dear."

Allison smiled so sweetly at him that Geoffrey gaped and the marquis paused, eyes widening in surprise. With a laugh of triumph, she kicked Blackie into a gallop and left them in the dust. As one, Geoffrey and the marquis set off after her.

Down the tree-lined lane they thundered. Allison knew the lane as well as Geoffrey did, and she had ridden Blackie for several years. Knowing both the territory and her mount so well, she easily kept the lead. She glanced back at the men galloping behind her and grinned saucily at them.

Geoffrey bent low over his horse's neck. He might not have the mighty Samson beneath him, but the white gelding was nearly as swift for the short run. Murmuring encouragement, he felt the beast stretch out, moving to the rhythm, flying down the lane leaving dust in his wake. He could feel the marquis at his heels and tried to focus only on catching Allison.

They neared the fork in the road. Allison slowed and took the turn with no more trouble than a slight leaning to one side. She glanced back again and saw Geoffrey pause only long enough to make sure the gelding knew his business before galloping after her. The marquis's Arabian took the corner as if it were born to it. Allison laughed in sheer delight and pressed her heels into Blackie's flanks.

Geoffrey could hear her laugh flung back at him as if in challenge and urged his gelding faster. Trees whipped past on either side in a golden blur. The dust from Allison's passing parted to let him through. Beneath him, the gelding shuddered and struggled to keep the pace.

Something white fluttered toward him, spooking the gelding for a moment. Geoffrey realized at the last second that it was the scarf that had held Allison's riding hat in place. Then it was past, and he was flying on. A moment later and he passed the blue-velvet hat at the side of the road.

Allison hadn't realized the scarf was loose, but she felt the hat topple down her back. It was gone before she could reach for it. Her mother would be furious. She grinned, bending low again. Let her be furious. Allison would help the groomsmen find the hat if she had to. This was entirely too much fun.

Behind her, Geoffrey bent low again, stroking the horse's neck and crooning encouragement. The gelding burst forward, steadily closing the distance between them and the flying black horse. They were ten yards behind, five yards, two yards. Feeling them so close, Allison glanced back and saw the gelding's head draw level with Blackie's flanks. Geoffrey raised his head and peered through the dust to catch sight of her. Like him, she had bent as well as she could in a sidesaddle. Her hair had come loose from its pins and streamed behind her in a banner of pale gold, bright against the black of the horse's mane and coat. She glanced back at him with an audacious grin and, with a cry, urged Blackie on.

They pounded into the clearing in front of the Abbey side by side, each turning in the opposite direction to slow their lathered mounts. He could see the grooms rushing from the stables and leapt from the saddle before the gelding had completely stopped. He hurried to Allison's side, and she beamed down at him.

"You are bested, sir!" she declared, eyes glowing and cheeks wind whipped.

"I confess myself laid low," he agreed, raising his arms to her. "May I assist the winner?"

"You may." Allison laughed, gathering her skirts together. She slid out of the sidesaddle and Geoffrey caught her waist, lowering her to the ground beside him. Her bosom heaved; her lips were pursed, begging to be kissed. He lowered his head without thinking.

Allison stared up at him, arrested. He was going to

kiss her. She closed her eyes and waited in eager expectation. Perhaps now she would see if Lady Janice's theory was true.

The marquis's horse galloped into the clearing, and Geoffrey froze scant inches from his goal. Blackie shied and he pulled Allison out of the way as she opened her eyes in surprise. She frowned at him, and he wondered if she realized how close he had come to losing control. The grooms dashed up to take the horses.

The marquis stepped forward, and Geoffrey belatedly realized he still held Allison by the waist. He let go and moved back. The marquis bowed to her and held out her hat and scarf.

"Well done, my dear." He smiled. "If you have another such victory, we are undone."

Allison accepted the hat and scarf with a nervous giggle. She told herself firmly she had no reason to feel guilty, but the feeling persisted. "You are too kind, my lord," she murmured.

"Kind, but last." He shrugged. "An excellent race, my dear. Pentercast, that was an interesting move you made toward the end. I wonder if you could explain it to me while I check my horse."

It was a command, not a request. There had been no move, Geoffrey was sure. But he couldn't very well call the man a liar in front of Allison. "With pleasure, my lord." He bowed.

"Excuse us, my dear." The marquis bowed in turn to Allison, who watched them wide-eyed. She had never heard the marquis sound so curt. She supposed he didn't like to lose, even to her, but she wondered whether something else might be bothering him.

Geoffrey fell into step beside him. "Was it the race or my treatment of Allison you found offensive?"

"Blunt and to the point," the marquis commented. "Very well, since you do not seem to value subtlety. You must have heard by now that Miss Munroe and I are engaged."

"I heard her mother agreed to the match," Geoffrey replied, struggling not to sound belligerent.

The marquis spared him a quick look. "And you do not think Miss Munroe favors my suit."

It was not his place to say so, even if he were sure it was still true. "You will have to ask Allison."

"Ah, yes, Allison. Allison is very lovely, very spirited, and very young. Do you think it fair to ask her to make such a momentous decision?"

"Whom are you protecting?" Geoffrey jeered. "Allison or yourself?"

The marquis went so far as to frown. "May I remind you that I am the injured party here? It was *my* fiancée you were attempting to kiss."

"And it was *my* love you got yourself affianced to!" Geoffrey countered.

The marquis stopped. "You fancy yourself in love with her?"

"With all my heart," Geoffrey declared, deciding he had nothing to lose.

"And I imagine you love as you ride—full of passion and recklessness."

"I would imagine," Geoffrey replied with no little pride.

The marquis nodded. "Excellent. It appears we shall have a noble battle then, and the winner shall have Miss Allison's heart."

Geoffrey frowned. "This isn't a contest."

"Isn't it?" the marquis countered. "You seemed to have made it so. Please don't think I mind, old fellow. I thrive on a good competition. But be advised. I rarely lose."

"Neither do I," Geoffrey assured him. "Neither do I."

Thirteen

From considering herself or everyone else mad, Allison quickly moved to annoyance. After the race, she was sure that Geoffrey was going to show his true stripes, but he returned to his cool civility almost immediately. True, it always seemed a bit strained now, particularly in front of the marquis. But that was only to be expected as the marquis's reticent demeanor seemed to have disappeared beneath a wave of competitiveness whose focus was Geoffrey Pentercast. She would have liked to return to some of her old past times with Geoffrey—riding, driving, helping some of the elderly parishioners. She wouldn't have minded if the marquis had wanted to continue his quiet courting. She could do none of those things. Geoffrey and the marquis were far too busy with each other to bother about her.

That it was jealousy was all too obvious, and that was perhaps what annoyed her most. She hadn't promised her heart to either of them, yet they both acted as if they were intent on protecting a particularly good hunting ground. They competed in everything around her. Geoffrey practically ran down the poor footman one afternoon in his attempt to reach her chair first and pull it out for her to sit. The marquis insisted on holding each platter of food as it was brought to her and picking out the delicacies that she might eat. The marquis resorted to reading the most suggestive of Shakespeare's love sonnets, but only if Geoffrey were in hearing distance. His impassioned reading only made her blush furiously and even succeeded in raising her mother's eyebrow. The first night he did so, Geoffrey tried serenading her in the moonlight outside her bedroom window, even though his bass voice was not at all suited for the melody he chose. The marquis countered with bringing her armloads of roses he had had his gardener send from the greenhouse of one of his estates. Geoffrey hadn't been able to top that right away, but what he chose to do instead was far worse in her mind. He had actually allowed her to win a horse race, obviously holding back Samson so that Blackie, who was less than half the horse, might win.

"This is getting ridiculous," she had hissed to him as he stood to help her down. Before he could respond, Samson had reared out of the waiting groom's hand, and Geoffrey had been forced to hurry over to calm the brute. The marquis had stepped smoothly into his place, arms outstretched.

"I quite agree with you, my dear," he said, as he lifted her easily to the ground. "Why don't you tell the oaf that you favor my suit, and we'll have done with all this nonsense?"

Allison had only glared at him.

Her one solace was that the days allotted for the marquis's visit were growing short. Up until he and Geoffrey had started this ridiculous competition, she would have said she had been growing fond of him. She still wasn't sure she could ever agree to marry him, but she had considered asking him to renew his courtship next Season. The winter in Wenwood would give her and the marquis time to think. It would also give her time to shake some sense into Geoffrey.

The final scheduled soirée was to be the Barnsley Assembly only a week before Guy Fawkes Day. All she had to do was to keep them at bay for a few days after that, and she would have the Abbey once more to herself.

She wasn't sure what to expect the night of the assembly. She was to ride in the marquis's carriage with her mother. Geoffrey, Genevieve, Alan, and the dowager Mrs. Pentercast were to meet them there. She dressed with little regard to what she wore, throwing on the blue dress from her come-out ball, but replacing the diamonds with the pearl necklace and earrings her father had given her on her fifteenth birthday and throwing a silvery gauze shawl about her shoulders. Her mother did not seem too pleased with her choice, raising a quizzing glass from the chest of her purple ball gown and squinting at her through it as if she had suddenly developed spots. The dismissive shake of her head as Perkins unobtrusively draped the black-velvet cloak about her shoulders did nothing to raise Allison's spirits.

She should not have been surprised to find two sets of flowers in the entryway of the Abbey that night. The magnificent white-rose corsage was from the marquis, with a card that read, "Only your beauty could dwarf such loveliness." Geoffrey had sent a nosegay of woodland violets with a card that bore only his initials. Both arrangements were lovely. However, she sadly decided, as she couldn't very well wear both and wearing either would have only given the advantage to one or the other, she elected to wear neither. Chimes bustled forward with her own velvet cloak, glaring at Perkins, whose noise raised fractionally higher. Allison set off to the assembly with only her pearls as decoration.

"I'd always thought it would be romantic to have two gentlemen fighting over me," she whispered to her sister Gen soon after they arrived. "But so help me, all I want to do is box their ears!"

Gen smiled sympathetically as she watched her husband dance with their mother. "Perhaps they'll be well-behaved tonight," she whispered back, absently rubbing her belly.

Allison regarded her sister with concern. "You look a little piqued. Are you and the baby all right?"

Gen smiled again. "Tolerable. Dr. Praxton says I seem to be coming along nicely. It is beginning to feel a bit ungainly. Mrs. Pentercast says I'm just about the size she was when she bore Alan. In fact, this lavender dress was one of hers. Even with her support, and yours, however, I probably shouldn't have come tonight. It's not as if I can dance."

Allison squeezed her hand. "But sometimes it's just enjoyable to be out with others. I'm glad you came."

"Thank you," Gen replied, returning the gesture. "Now, let us hope your two suitors behave so that we both might have a good time."

But their hopes were dashed almost immediately. The marquis and Geoffrey seemed intent on showing each other up. The marquis, in a splendid black coat and breeches and sapphire waistcoat that would have graced any London ball, made sure to claim Allison's hand for the second set. Geoffrey, looking only slightly less sartorial in his black coat, gray breeches, and navy figured waistcoat, had claimed her afterward and kept her on the floor two dances in a row, raising several eyebrows in the process. The marquis capped him by getting the widow Munroe to dance on the parquet floor while many of the villagers of Wenwood and Barnsley watched from wide walkways and scattered chairs and divans. Allison had hoped that having them both on the floor would give her a few minutes in which to have a private word with Geoffrey. To her dismay, he coerced the elderly widow Tate to dance instead. She wasn't entirely sure what that was supposed to prove, unless it was how

gentlemanly he had become. She surrendered herself to
Alan and tried to enjoy the dance.

Their competition only worsened as the night wore
on. Geoffrey was first to bring her refreshments from
the laden table on one side of the large, open room,
but it was the marquis who brought her the little iced
cakes to which she was partial. The marquis promenaded with her about the room, but Geoffrey found her
a seat on one of the divans on which to rest afterward.
If she hadn't been so annoyed by all the attention to
pointless details, she was sure she would have found it
all very funny.

Geoffrey was also not finding the situation very funny.
Try as he might, he couldn't seem to outdo the marquis. To be fair, he supposed, the man had had a number of years more experience than Geoffrey at this sort
of thing; but even when Geoffrey managed to move the
situation to something more active like riding or dancing, the man still showed to advantage. As fierce as they
had been all night, he was, therefore, surprised when
the marquis tapped him on the shoulder and motioned
him to a quiet corner of the assembly hall.

"Are you quite through?" he demanded, blue eyes
smoldering.

Geoffrey tried not to rejoice at this sign that he might
actually be getting to the man. "Never," he swore. "You
wanted a contest, my lord. You shall have it until one
of us is chosen victor."

The marquis's jaw tightened. "I won't let you have
her. You're not worthy of her."

Geoffrey grinned at him. "That is for Allison to decide. Now if you'll excuse me, I have pressing business
with the string quartet."

He could feel the peer frowning at him as he saun-
tered away.

Across the assembly hall, Allison stood beside her

mother, resting for a moment from the dances. She knew she should be enjoying herself. The music was fine, there were plenty of young gentlemen with which to dance, and the cool autumn air coming through the open doors on the far wall kept the crowded hall at a reasonable temperature. If only the marquis and Geoffrey had been behaving. If only her mother would speak to her rather than to complain of her own behavior. If only wishes were kittens.

"What do you think about that dress Mary Delacourte is wearing?" her mother asked her.

Allison blinked, surprised and gratified at being asked for an opinion. She stared at her mother openmouthed for a moment, then hurriedly tried to find the tall young woman who had lived near them since they were children. "It's a lovely shade of purple," she ventured, spying her among a crowd of gentlemen across from them, "but it makes her look old."

Her mother nodded. "My thoughts entirely. Purple is a color for matrons. I much prefer the blues you affect."

Allison beamed. "Thank you, Mother."

Her mother snapped open her fan and applied it gently. "And has the marquis mentioned how he is enjoying his stay with us?"

"He appears to be enjoying it quite well," Allison all but snapped.

Her mother raised an eyebrow. "You do not sound pleased. It seemed to me that you two were getting on rather well."

Allison sighed, putting on a pleasant smile that she knew would satisfy her mother. "We had been getting on famously. But he has been preoccupied of late." She couldn't very well complain about Geoffrey to her mother. The widow Munroe would only have refused to allow him to call. Even as annoyed as Allison was with him, she didn't like the idea of his disappearing entirely.

That made her realize she had lost sight of both him and the marquis among the crowds. She turned to face her mother in time to see her actually chewing her lower lip. She was so surprised that she almost forget what she was going to say. She collected her thoughts with difficulty. "Do you see the marquis about, Mother?"

Before her mother could answer, both the marquis and Geoffrey appeared beside her. "All this standing about after dancing must have chilled you, Miss Munroe," Geoffrey mused, all solicitation, although his eyes never left the marquis beside him. "Perhaps you'd like that fetching shawl you were wearing earlier?"

"Splendid idea, Pentercast," the marquis replied before Allison could assert that she was perfectly fine. "Allow me to get it for you, my dear." He was off before she or Geoffrey could stop him.

Geoffrey scowled. Allison was ready to tell him to stop this ridiculous behavior when his brow cleared. He nodded toward the top of the room where the trio of musicians was beginning the strains of the next dance.

"About time," he declared. "I've been after them to play a waltz all night." He held out his hands and offered her a wink that made her heart sing. "Come on, moonling; let's show them how it's done."

He was so much like the Geoffrey of old, eyes twinkling with mischief, head cocked in challenge, that she couldn't deny him. With a laugh, she took his hands and let him lead her onto the floor.

Neither of them was all that good at waltzing, she realized as they bumbled about the room. It wasn't too surprising, she supposed. She had only seen it done a few times, and only practiced it once in the kitchen of the London town house. Of course, there were no tables or chairs to steer around on the floor of Barnsley Grange as there had been in London. In fact, Allison realized after a few turns, there weren't even any other couples to watch for. Everyone had cleared the floor for her and Geoffrey.

She felt a surge of pride as he grinned at her. They were dancing so beautifully that everyone else was obviously content to stand aside and watch. She threw herself into the movements with renewed vigor, and Geoffrey laughed out loud as he twirled her about. She'd never felt so perfectly at ease, as if this were where she belonged. Gazing up into those dark-brown eyes, she suddenly realized that the feelings of exuberance had less to do with the dance and far more to do with the fact that she was in Geoffrey Pentercast's arms. The very thought made her stumble. Geoffrey caught her effortlessly and swept her back into step.

She knew her face must be a flaming red as the music ended, somewhat abruptly she thought. They swung to a stop. Geoffrey released her and bowed. She remembered to curtsey. As she rose, she realized that everyone in the room was staring. Just as quickly as the blood had risen to her cheeks, it left. What she had taken for admiration was shock. She did not need to turn her head to know her mother was bearing down on her.

"You were magnificent," Geoffrey murmured beside her, seeing the approaching juggernaut. "Don't let them take that away from you."

Allison swallowed, turning. Beside her mother strode the marquis. She felt herself stiffen at the fire in his eye. Before she could speak, however, he stopped to drape the shawl over her shoulders.

"Quite an exhibition, my dear," he said loudly enough to be overheard by all the dowagers nearby, including a wide-eyed Mrs. Pentercast. All the dowagers leaned forward as they caught the whiff of gossip. "Your grace on the dance floor is ever inspiring."

"Thank you, my lord," she managed, keeping her eyes lowered.

"In fact, I am so proud of your accomplishments that I can wait no longer to make our announcement."

Allison gasped, head coming up involuntarily. His jaw was set, his blue eyes icy with implacability. "You wouldn't. Not here, not now."

"You've left me with little choice if I am to win this game," he replied coldly.

"Don't," Geoffrey said quietly. "We all know it's a lie."

The marquis's face hardened still more. "You were amusing, Pentercast. You are amusing no longer. I find I have no more patience for this competition."

"No one asked you to compete in the first place," Allison interrupted heatedly.

"My lord," Mrs. Munroe put in. "This is not seemly. We are making a scene. I believe we would be better served to make the announcement before a select group of friends and family, as you agreed."

"I find I have changed my mind," he replied, refusing to look at her. He raised his voice. "Pardon me, gentle people, but I have an announcement to make."

Allison grasped his arm. "Please, Thomas, don't do this. I will only have to deny you publicly."

"You wouldn't dare," he all but sneered. "Your mother has given her word."

"Then, sir," Allison replied firmly, refusing to quail before his fury, "you may marry my mother."

"Enough," her mother snapped. Allison stared at her in amazement. She raised her voice. "Friends, neighbors, pardon this intrusion, as the marquis has requested, but we do, indeed, have most joyous news."

"Mother!" Allison cried.

"It is my pleasure to announce . . ."

"Don't!"

". . . the engagement . . ."

"Stop!"

". . . of my daughter Allison . . ."

"I refuse!"

". . . to the Marquis DeGuis."

In desperation, Allison reached out a hand to Geoffrey. He started forward only to be swept aside by the tide of well-wishers who engulfed them. Allison struggled against them, ignoring the outstretched arms, the smiling faces, the cries of delight. She felt as if she were drowning, suffocating, being trampled. Someone grabbed her arm, and she found herself facing her mother, who enfolded her in a fierce hug.

"It's for the best, dearest," she murmured in Allison's ear. "You'll see. Everything is arranged, you see . . . the church, the flowers, your dress. If I hadn't stepped in, you might have married someone like Geoffrey Pentercast."

"Oh, Mother!" Allison started to cry. "Can't you see? That's exactly what I should be doing!"

Fourteen

Geoffrey sat in the Pentercast carriage and glowered. He was frustrated, angry, and confused. He did not need to be told that his face reflected his feelings, for his mother had retreated as far away from him as the velvet-upholstered seat they shared in the landau would permit. Her tiny face was puckered in motherly concern. Across from them, Gen was eyeing him with obvious sympathy, and Alan had a frown that must nearly match his own.

"You all think this is over, don't you?" he growled at them.

Alan and Genevieve exchanged glances, which only served to fuel his fire. "I'm sorry, old man," Alan offered. "The choice has always been Miss Allison's. I just didn't think this would be the final outcome."

Geoffrey snorted. "It isn't the final outcome. Not if I have anything to say about it."

"That's just it, dearest," Genevieve put in gently. "You haven't anything to say about it. It does seem as if Allison has made her choice."

"I don't believe it!" Geoffrey declared, frustration packing every syllable.

His mother's eyes widened. "But it was announced, in public. Surely you heard Trudy."

"We all heard my mother," Genevieve assured her mother-in-law. "I have to own I find it as odd as Geoffrey does. I was in a position to see Allison's face as Mother made the announcement. She was anguished."

"There." Geoffrey nodded, glaring at his mother to disprove it. She merely frowned back at him, mouth pursed thoughtfully.

"But it will not be easy to get out of so public an announcement," she insisted. "No young lady likes to be termed a jilt, even a Munroe."

Genevieve's eyes narrowed, but Geoffrey had to admire the fact that she chose not to remind her mother-in-law that she had been a Munroe until less than a year ago. "Allison isn't a jilt," she sniffed.

"Not if she doesn't refuse the Marquis DeGuis," Mrs. Pentercast agreed brightly.

"Even if she does refuse the Marquis DeGuis," Geoffrey maintained belligerently. His mother pouted, turning her face to the window.

"I truly don't know what to think." Genevieve sighed. "It has seemed to me that Allison really wasn't sure which of you to choose. Have you done anything recently, Geoffrey, to sway her toward the marquis?"

"Nothing," Geoffrey said quellingly. "And I cannot believe Allison would allow me to hear it first in public like that. She would have told me to my face that she preferred someone else."

Alan nodded. "You have a point there. I've never known your sister, Gen, to go behind someone's back with news of this importance."

Genevieve nodded as well. "I quite agree. But if Allison didn't agree to the marquis's suit, what on earth possessed Mother to announce it that way?"

"She's preening, of course." The dowager Mrs. Pentercast sniffed, turning to face them once more. "She's been on her high ropes ever since she brought that man back from town. Her older daughter may have settled for a country squire, but Miss Allison was going to be a *lady*."

Geoffrey scowled. "So, she was hanging out for the title, was she?"

"Geoffrey," Gen said warningly. She turned to her mother-in-law. "I think you do my mother an injustice, Mother Pentercast. Allison told me how she agreed to the engagement without Allison's knowledge, but surely she wouldn't have announced it in public without some indication from Allison."

"I don't want to argue with you, dear," Mrs. Pentercast replied firmly. "I suppose you'll just have to ask your mother." She turned away again, but not before muttering under her breath, "If you can get a word in around her bragging."

Geoffrey ignored his mother, as Gen was apparently trying to do. Mrs. Pentercast and Mrs. Munroe had competed since childhood—who would be the first to wed, who would catch the richest prize on the marriage mart, who would bear the first son. It was natural for his mother to assume the widow Munroe was still competing. Geoffrey was afraid there was more to it than that.

"That still does not explain the marquis's behavior," Genevieve continued. "He has always impressed me as such a private man. Whatever made him want to announce the engagement so suddenly like that?"

Geoffrey shook his head, gazing out the window into the darkness beyond the carriage lights. "I drove him to it. I simply couldn't leave well enough alone. I thought I could actually win at this civil game we've been playing. What a fool!"

"Courting can be a game, Geoffrey," Genevieve replied quietly, "but it need not be. I don't think it was a game to Allison."

"Then why didn't she do more than that half-hearted attempt to resist?" he demanded, turning to her.

Gen recoiled at the anger in his face, and Alan's arm slid around her shoulders as if in protection.

Geoffrey ran his hand back through his hair. "I'm sorry. I didn't mean to take my anger out on you. But the simple matter is, your sister allowed herself to become engaged with no more than a momentary struggle. As you said, she'll not get out of this easily."

And why should she even try, his better half argued as he returned his gaze to the darkness. In the last few weeks, he had developed a grudging admiration for the Marquis DeGuis. The man was clever and generally good-natured, with a quiet sense of humor that was all the more enjoyable because it showed so rarely. He was a bruising rider, an excellent shot, and a brilliant billiard player. Although Geoffrey hadn't succeeded in getting him drunk the few nights they had sat over port after dinner, he had no doubt that the marquis would be a friendly drunk. In all things, the marquis seemed the sort of man Geoffrey had always wanted to be. He had never thought the man would prove to have such a marked jealous streak.

Which only meant that he had been close to reaching his goal, Geoffrey realized in the silence the followed their conversation. Why else would the marquis show his hand like that unless he was sure he was losing? The announcement would make Geoffrey's job all that much harder, he knew. But even if Allison earned the name of jilt for a time, he was sure it wouldn't matter once she was his wife. That still left him with his original goals—convince Allison and convince Mrs. Munroe that he was a better catch than the marquis.

The carriage trundled up the drive to the manor. His mother stirred beside him, shaking out her black velvet evening cloak in preparation of alighting. Genevieve did likewise, grimacing as her shifting brought her belly up against Alan's waist. Geoffrey eyed her.

"I know you must be tired, Genevieve, but may I have a word with you before you retire?"

Alan frowned at him but did not gainsay his wife as she nodded. Mrs. Pentercast yawned.

"Oh, my dears, I'm quite done in. Geoffrey, try not to fret, dear. As I've said many times, the Munroe women are not capable of understanding love as we know it."

Now it was Geoffrey's turn to frown as the footmen helped them alight. Alan was quick to hold Gen's hand as she carefully stepped from the carriage, murmuring assurances that he found a certain ex-Munroe quite capable of understanding love.

His mother's remark gave Geoffrey a moment alone in the darkness. Mrs. Munroe was known for her coolness, but Allison? There was nothing cold or restrained about Allison, or at least there hadn't been before she had left for London. Had a Season so changed her that she no longer felt comfortable displaying her feelings? Certainly she had seemed reticent since she had returned. If it were true, he had misjudged her reactions badly.

Still deep in thought, he wandered into the manor and allowed Munson, their butler, to steer him toward the sitting room off the spacious entry where Genevieve awaited him. She was just lowering herself onto the settee, with what seemed like great difficulty to him. He shook himself and hurried to her other side to assist Alan.

"I'm fine." She smiled at them both as she was seated. "Alan, you must stop fussing, and Geoffrey, you mustn't let Alan convince you that fussing is necessary."

Geoffrey grinned, going to sit on the chair opposite her even as his brother sank onto the settee beside her. "You're wasting your breath. Alan lives to fuss over those he loves."

Alan smiled ruefully. "I never thought of it as fussing, if you please. Besides, how many times in life does a man become a father for the first time?"

Gen shook her head fondly. "Obviously not enough." She turned her attention to Geoffrey. "Now, I assume you wanted to continue our conversation about Allison?"

"Yes," Geoffrey admitted. "When we started this escapade, you offered to speak to your mother on my behalf. I take it you've done so, to no avail."

Gen smiled at him fondly. "I have, my dear. You must be realistic, Geoffrey. What mother would prefer a second son just starting his life to a peer of the realm with estates spread from one end of the empire to the other?"

Geoffrey frowned, frustration building again. "Then I have no chance of winning her over?"

"Not from that angle," Gen agreed. She started to lean forward, remembered her stomach, and grimaced, straightening. Geoffrey stopped himself from asking if she were all right. She had just finished scolding him for fussing, as she called it. She wouldn't welcome another comment so soon.

"However," she was continuing, "there is one hope for you. If Allison declares her love for you, I don't think Mother will gainsay her."

"So," Geoffrey mused, "you're saying that the only person I have to convince of my worthiness is Allison."

Genevieve nodded. "Exactly. I wish I could offer you more advice than that, Geoffrey, but I don't know how Allison feels. She told me tonight that she was ready to strangle you both."

"Why?" Geoffrey frowned. "What have I done to displease her?"

"You and the marquis have been both a bit competitive the last few weeks, don't you think?" Genevieve asked with an upraised eyebrow.

When Geoffrey scowled at her, Alan jumped in. "Oh, come now, old man. You both have been making cakes of yourselves. I thought I was going to suffocate from the perfume in church last Sunday from all the flowers you two had donated in Miss Allison's honor. It's a wonder Reverend Wellfordhouse could give his sermon without sneezing himself to death."

"And did you have to carve her initials into every tree in the orchard?" Genevieve put in. "Mrs. Gurney came by to tell me we had some sort of disease among our trees when she saw the marks on the way to the village."

Geoffrey hung his head, suddenly feeling foolish. "I suppose it was a bit much."

"Much too much," Genevieve maintained. "Is it any wonder Allison wanted to wash her hands of the pair of you?"

"Yet she agreed to marry the marquis," Alan mused.

"We don't know that," Geoffrey snapped, rising to pace. "I wish you would all stop assuming the worst."

"The announcement certainly seems binding," Genevieve allowed, "but truly, it is only as good as Allison allows it to be. She can still change her mind."

Geoffrey snorted. "And everyone seems certain she won't do that. You said it yourself: The marquis is perfect."

"And as you said, Allison isn't one to prefer perfection." She tapped her chin thoughtfully with one finger. "I cannot stop thinking about how miserable Allison looked when Mother made the announcement. She hated what was happening. I don't think she will go through with it, Geoffrey. I don't think she loves the marquis."

"Even so, it does not follow that she, therefore, loves

me," Geoffrey countered. He took a few turns around the sofa, thinking of what else he could possibly do to prove his love to her. If Gen was right, his actions the last few weeks had only served to annoy Allison. It sounded as if he had lost ground rather than gained it. He was on his third circuit when he noticed that Gen was straining to follow his movements, face contorted in discomfort. Sheepishly, he hastily returned to his seat.

"So, what would you advise?" he prompted his sister-in-law.

Genevieve eyed him, then glanced back at Alan.

Geoffrey narrowed his eyes. "I realize you two are husband and wife, but could you please stop sharing thoughts in front of me? It's damned annoying."

"Watch your language," Alan growled, hand once more protectively on Gen's shoulder. Gen put her hand over his and faced Geoffrey.

"I think the time is right for a bold act, Geoffrey," she proclaimed.

Geoffrey raised an eyebrow. "A bold act? Genevieve, are you encouraging me to behave in an uncivil manner?"

Her eyes twinkled, and suddenly he thought he understood why his brother had married her. "Heaven forbid, my dear! You have proven yourself every bit as refined and polished as the Marquis DeGuis." She glanced back at Alan again, then grinned at Geoffrey. "Perhaps it's time you proved yourself a Pentercast."

Fifteen

Allison had a great deal of time to think how she should react to her mother's betrayal. She knew Geoffrey had been disappointed that she had not cried out against the injustice right there at the ball. She could see the accusations in those deep-brown eyes of his. But if this Season had taught her anything, it was that sometimes it was better to think before reacting. She knew that this was one of those times.

The widow Munroe was just as confused as Geoffrey had been that she did not react. By the light of the lanterns outside the carriage she could see her mother casting her glances, brow creased in thought. She wondered what her mother expected—tears? Shouted refusals? Threats of escape or retribution? None of those things would solve the problem that had been thrust upon her.

Her future had been declared publicly. Now, should she refuse the marquis's offer, she would not only cause her mother to break her word but she would humiliate both her mother and the marquis. It was no more than they deserved for treating her so cavalierly, but she could not find it in her to be so vengeful. For all the widow Munroe's misplaced notions, her mother was only trying to ensure a future for her daughter. And the marquis did earnestly want her for his wife. Their motives were honorable even if she abhorred their methods of acting on them.

The marquis watched her as well, his gaze traveling between her and her mother. There was something in the darting glances that reminded her of a child caught in some mischief and unsure of the punishment. Even he did not seem to know what to make of her silence. She was hurt enough that she let them stew. She wasn't sure what to say to them anyway.

Perkins whisked open the doors as they alighted, his stiffly proper bow earning him no more than a cursory glance from her mother as she handed him her cloak. Allison paused to wonder where Chimes had gotten to, but she caught her mother approaching and purposely turned her back, letting one of the hovering footmen take her own wraps. As soon as he was finished, she moved to continue on to her room, head high. The marquis touched her arm, slowing her.

"Shouldn't we talk, Miss Munroe?" he asked, rather shakily she thought.

"Yes, my lord, we should," she replied, refusing to be swayed by the hangdog expression on his handsome face. "But now is neither the time nor the place. We will all be better served if we sleep on the issue. Good night. Good night, Mother."

Both her mother and the marquis murmured appropriate farewells and she left them in the entryway looking bewildered.

She wasn't sure whether she'd sleep at all that night, but a strange sort of peace had fallen over her and she was asleep almost immediately upon lying on the four-poster bed. When she awoke at a fashionably late hour, she was just as calm. Perhaps her Season had taught her something, she mused as she dressed herself in her darkest blue dress, a navy kerseymere with a white lace collar and cuffs. Mary poked her head in during the process, and Allison accepted the platter of meat she carried and waved her away. She wanted to be alone with this feeling of personal power. She opened the ornamental cage and fed Pippin on her lap.

When the little fellow had finished, she stroked his soft fur for a few moments before returning him to his home. She'd been in a cage like his, within the bars her mother had erected. Even though her mother had carefully crafted them, Allison had been the one to agree to live within them. Like Pippin, she kept trying to escape, only to be returned. Today, she determined, that escape would be permanent.

She sat at her dressing table and ran the silver-backed brush through her flaxen hair, flattening her usual ringlets until she could catch the hair up in a bun at the nape of her neck. The woman gazing back at her looked stern and matronly—a governess, perhaps, or the housekeeper of a huge estate. She nodded in approval and rose to go to the kitchen.

Chimes was sitting at the oak worktable in the center of the kitchen, a newspaper the marquis's man-of-affairs had sent several days ago open before him. "Chimes," Allison announced as she sailed into the room, "you were not on duty last night."

The man-of-all-work snapped shut the paper and glowered at her. "You saying I was actually missed? Ha!"

Allison returned his scowl, her feeling of control singing in her veins. "Of course you were missed. You run this household, do you not?"

He frowned at her, then craned his neck to peer more closely. "You feeling all right this morning, Miss Allison?"

"Perfectly fine," Allison replied, nose in the air. "Annie, would you possibly have time to make me tea and biscuits? I'm starving."

"I'll make you a whole breakfast," the little housekeeper promised, shaking out the crisp white apron that covered her black bombazine. As long as Allison had known her, Annie had never so much as stained the white apron. Now the woman hurried over to the stove across the room, humming as she selected the correct pots and pans from a rack overhead. "They've been up for hours," she confided over her shoulder. "Gossip has it your engagement was announced at the assembly. Neither of them looked all too pleased about it, Miss Allison."

Allison smiled wryly. "I hope neither of them slept well."

Chimes grinned. "Sounds like you have them right where you want them, Miss Allison."

She felt an answering grin tugging at the corners of her mouth. "Sounds like you're right." She winked at him. "What do you think I should ask for in atonement?"

"Oh, Miss Allison," Annie scolded, "you wouldn't use your poor mother so."

"Hush, woman," Chimes grumbled. "She knows what she's about." He motioned Allison closer. "You stand your ground, girl," he hissed when she had bent her ear to him. "You've done nothing to be ashamed of. You just remember that."

The words echoed Geoffrey's warning of the night before, and gooseflesh rose on her arms even as her feeling of power threatened to collapse. Her sudden fears must have showed on her face, for Chimes covered her hand on the table with one of his own. "You'll be fine, gel. Remember who you are. You're Rutherford Munroe's daughter, aren't you? Give them hell."

Allison nodded, swallowing. "I'll try, Chimes. Thank you."

He nodded as well, pulling his hand away. Annie bustled to lay a place beside him at the table for Allison.

"On the other hand"—she smiled brightly—"perhaps you might suggest that when the marquis goes he take that beanpole of a butler with him."

Allison glanced at Chimes, who suddenly found his dirty nails of great interest. "Haven't you been able to put that man in his place?"

Chimes snorted. "I put him there often enough. Seems he doesn't know enough to stay there."

"I hate the thought of him living here with us." Allison frowned. "You two are like family. I would never feel that way about Perkins."

Chimes's eyes narrowed. "Family, eh? Kind of you to say so, Miss Allison. Perhaps that's just the ticket to send his highness meandering back to London."

"What are you going to do?" Allison demanded, not sure whether to be amused or concerned by the gleam in the man's eye.

Chimes shrugged, rising. "Not sure yet. You'll see when the time comes. Just you make sure you put your mum in *her* place."

Allison grinned at him. "I'll try, Chimes."

Sometime later, well-fed and buoyed with support, Allison found her way to the music room, where she could hear her mother playing at the spinet. The melancholy notes echoed down the hall, enhancing the chill of fall that seemed to be permeating through the stone walls. She hoped the sounds were indications of her mother's remorse over her behavior last evening, but then she wasn't sure she remembered her mother ever playing a happy tune. With a sigh, she straightened her shoulders and entered the room.

At least the music room was a comfortable place. She and Gen had been want to retreat there to share confidences and practice being ladies. It was a small room, the walls hung in ivory satin. The main furnishing was an old sofa pressed between two floor-to-ceiling bookcases that held a number of musical scores her father had had loosely bound as well as her sister's and her favorite books. The only other piece in the room was the spinet piano on the far wall.

Her mother looked up from concentrating on the music as Allison entered, her gaze thoughtful. Allison was rather surprised to see that the marquis was with her. He stood by the single slitted window the room possessed, gazing out at the front yard as if he had been expecting someone. Her mother, she saw, was dressed in one of the dresses from her time of mourning, the black silk rustling as she moved to turn a page of the music. The marquis was also dressed in a black coat and trousers. Allison shook her head at their weary faces. She was the one who'd been manipulated out of a future. What had they to be so glum about?

"I believe it's my turn to make an announcement," she declared, moving into the room.

Her mother stopped playing immediately. The marquis stiffened, turning to face her fully.

She ought to let them dangle just a few more minutes, she thought. Lady Janice certainly would have done so. But again, her heart would not allow her to be so unkind.

"Lord DeGuis," she continued, knowing she had their full attention. "I thank you for the great honor you have done me in offering for my hand. I would wager every young lady in London would give up vouchers to Almack's to stand in my shoes. You have been kind, chivalrous, and attentive. You are everything I thought I ever wanted in a husband, but I find I simply cannot marry a man who would go back on a promise."

"I see," he replied calmly. "And are you not at all concerned about the gossip that might ensue after last night's announcement?"

It was not a threat; she could see by the frown in his

eyes that he was genuinely concerned about it. "Not overly concerned," she told him truthfully. "Young ladies are allowed to change their minds. I believe it is called *crying off.*"

"I believe," her mother said in a stilted voice, "that it is called *jilting.*"

She smiled sweetly at her mother. "Call it what you like, Mother. It will not deter me."

"It is your decision, Miss Munroe," the marquis put in, giving Mrs. Munroe a determined frown that only made her shrink more into herself. "Your reputation stands to be damaged more than anyone's."

Mrs. Munroe's head jerked up and she stared at him. "Then you will not hold me to my promise?" she gasped.

Allison watching with interest as the marquis bowed to her. "No, madame. I can see now it was a bad choice to begin with. I had always thought it proper to deal with the lady's family first; but in the case of a strong-willed lady like your daughter, it was an insult to go to anyone but her." He turned to bow to Allison. "And I must also apologize for my actions last night, Miss Munroe. My temper has a long fuse; but once it reaches the powder, it can cause a great deal of damage. I'm afraid I let my jealousy of Mr. Pentercast get the better of me. It was wrong of me to put you on the spot."

Allison eyed him suspiciously. "I must confess that I find it hard to believe this sudden capitulation. Do you really give in so easily?"

He chuckled. "I doubt you'd rather I denied all wrongdoing and demanded you marry me. I admire you, too much to force you into anything. I still stand on my opinion that you would make an excellent marchioness. If there is anything I can do or say to make you change your mind . . ."

Allison held up her hand to stop him. "You will have

to go a long way to do so, my lord. You made a promise to me that the decision was to be mine and mine alone. In my opinion, you had little right to be jealous and less to allow it to goad you into breaking a promise."

He swallowed. "I begin to see why some people call you forthright."

She shrugged. "Better you know now than later. I believe I actually owe you an apology there. I admit the honor of being courted by you was a bit overwhelming. You didn't get much of a chance to know the real me either."

"I disagree," he replied. "From the first I admired your spirit, Miss Munroe. It was my mistake to think that what that spirit needed was a firm hand." He stepped toward her and offered her his hand. "Can we not start over? I promise to be a model suitor."

Allison grimaced. "I am quite fed up with model anythings, my lord. Is it not possible for us to be friends?"

"Friends," he mused. He eyed her for a moment and she thought he meant to argue. She straightened and returned his look boldly. "Friends, then," he agreed. "Given that, perhaps it would be best if I stayed at an inn until I can make arrangements to return to London."

"You do not have to do that on my account," Allison replied. "Mother?"

Her mother shook herself. "That is not necessary, my lord. You are most welcome to stay."

He bowed again. "Thank you both. It would make things easier. It shouldn't take me more than a day or two to make all the arrangements."

"Take as long as you need," Mrs. Munroe assured him.

"If you'll excuse me, I'll get right to it." He nodded to them both and quit the room.

"That was a grave error, Allison." Her mother sighed.

"No, Mother," Allison replied firmly. "The grave error was yours."

Her mother stiffened, but Allison continued before she could lose heart. "I cannot believe you did not trust me to make my own decisions. Everything I did this Season was to show you I had grown up. I'm sorry you didn't notice. But I won't put myself on display for you again. This is my life to live as I see fit. If I cannot do it here with you, I will do it elsewhere."

Her mother pursed her lips. "Don't be silly. Where would you go?"

"To live with Gen perhaps? Or maybe the vicar could find me a position as a governess. I've always liked children."

Her mother shuddered. "I will not have you living as a servant."

"You have no choice in the matter," Allison declared. "Or rather, you do have a choice—treat me with the respect I think you know in your heart I've earned or watch me walk out the door. I love you, Mother, but it is my life and it is high time I started acting like it."

Sixteen

As it turned out, Allison did not have to make good on her threats that day. Her mother was sufficiently depressed about the entire state of affairs that no more was said regarding the potential of her marrying the marquis. In fact, the widow Munroe retired to her room for the rest of the day, leaving Allison alone to her thoughts.

The quiet of the Abbey did not last long, however. Early afternoon brought a visit from Genevieve, who was helped into the Abbey by Chimes. Allison had come into the entryway at the sound of a carriage on the drive. Perkins was notably absent, as he always seemed to be when her mother wasn't there to admire his posturing. Allison hurried to help escort her sister.

"Will you all stop hovering over me?" Gen complained after she had been seated on the music room sofa. She eased the skirts of the saffron dress over her middle. "Honestly, you would think I was having the baby right now!"

"Well, it won't be long by the look of you," Chimes countered, wiping sweat from his brow with a handkerchief. "What does Dr. Praxton say?"

"Three to four more weeks," Gen all but groaned. Allison smiled in sympathy. Chimes hurried out to find her some refreshments.

"Well?" Gen demanded. "Are you going to let them get away with it?"

Allison grinned. "No, and I've already told them so."

"Ah," Gen nodded. "And that would explain why Mother is in bed with the megrims."

"Yes," Allison sighed. "I truly don't want to hurt her, Gen, but I cannot let her manage my life like this."

"No, indeed," her sister replied supportively. "And what will you do now?"

"I wish I knew!" Allison sighed again. "I suppose I have to go through it all again next Season, don't I?"

"Unless you've found the man of your dreams."

Allison didn't like the way her sister said that; it was entirely too sure. "What do you mean? Don't tell me you think I should marry the marquis, too?"

"Not the marquis," Gen hedged, avoiding her eye. "I understand you had many suitors, Allison. Did none of them stir your blood?"

Allison jumped to her feet impatiently. "What is all this about stirring the blood? You talk just like Lady Janice. Must a man turn you into a lump of charcoal with the fire of his passion to make it a good marriage?"

"Nothing so dramatic as that." Gen laughed. "I don't know what your friend Lady Janice said, dearest, but I must admit I think I realized I loved Alan the day he kissed me."

Allison sank back into her seat, bemused. "Really? Is a kiss of such importance then?"

Her sister shrugged. "For some. I think what's really important is that you love the gentleman. I find it hard to imagine Alan without his kiss, but I know I loved him before the kiss made me realize it. Does that make sense?"

"No." Allison sighed. "Or rather, perhaps. I suppose I won't know until I've been kissed."

"Well, I wouldn't paint a sign to that effect," Gen

teased her. "I can think of several gentlemen who would be only too glad to demonstrate the joys of kissing, Geoffrey, for one."

"Geoffrey!" Allison cried, jumping to her feet again. She could feel the color draining from her face. "Oh, Gen, how could I have forgotten! What must he think of me for not letting him know that I refused the engagement?"

Her sister smiled. "I think he'll be delighted with the news, love, if you don't mind if I share it."

"Yes, of course, please do. The sooner people know the truth of the matter, the better."

"And what," her sister said carefully, "exactly is the truth of the matter?"

Allison paced about the room. "I think I understand your concern. We will be making gossip, won't we?"

"I'm afraid so, love." Gen sighed. "But I agree with you that the sooner everyone knows the truth, the less difficult it will be. Perhaps you and the marquis can agree on a likely story."

Allison nodded. "That would probably be best. I'll talk to him later today."

"And when you do so, perhaps you can ask him something else as well," her sister put in.

"Oh?" Allison prompted politely.

"Alan has planned a rather large event for Guy Fawkes Day," Gen confessed. "There'll be feasting and fireworks and a bonfire behind the manor. Of course, we had no idea the marquis would put you in this awkward position when we made the arrangements. Do you think you can bring yourself to be seen in public only two days from now?"

"For a party such as that—" Allison grinned. "—I shall make every effort."

Gen smiled back. "Now you just need to convince Mother."

"I do not have to convince Mother of anything," Allison replied heatedly. "I believe I have just proven that. However, I will ask her whether she wishes to come with me."

Gen eyed her sister for a moment and Allison wondered what was going through her mind. "Will the marquis still be about?"

"And why do you say that in such a calculating manner?" Allison asked suspiciously. "I warn you, Gen, I've been pushed farther than I ever intend to be pushed again. Do not try to get me to see the marquis in a better light."

Gen put her hand over her heart. "I? I would never do anything so underhanded."

Allison did not like the twinkle in those blue eyes. "Just see that you do not," she warned. "I'd be delighted to attend your Guy Fawkes Day party, and I will ask the marquis whether he would like to attend, but I will go no farther."

"I wouldn't dream of asking you to do more than that," Gen assured her. "But I know it will mean a great deal to Geoffrey if you come."

Allison felt herself blushing. "I hope you won't force him at me either, Gen. I need to understand my own heart first."

Her sister nodded. "I understand. If it helps any, dear, I think he cares for you deeply."

Allison sighed. "That's what I'm afraid of."

She thought for some time that afternoon after her sister made her ponderous way home. It seemed to her that perhaps Lady Janice was right: A kiss did indeed hold the key to how one felt about a gentleman. She knew she wouldn't have to ask Geoffrey twice for a kiss. But she caught herself wondering what it would be like to kiss the marquis. Would his kiss be as cool and collected as the man? Or would it give her insight into his feelings as well as her own? She had been prepared to send him packing for the way he had broken his promise to her. But was she making a mistake as her mother thought? He was the catch of the Season. Perhaps she should give him another chance.

She was still mulling it over when she met her mother and the marquis in the dining room for dinner that night. The marquis reported that he had posted several letters, but he wasn't sure how long it would take for them to reach his man-of-affairs or for his other estates to be made ready for his return. He was very polite about it, but Allison had the sneaking suspicion that he was not trying overly hard to quit Wenwood Abbey. She watched him throughout the meal, but she saw no sign that he and her mother were plotting anything. She wished she could trust them both. It would have made her decisions much easier.

She continued to watch him the next day when she was afforded the opportunity. He spent the morning closeted in the library with his estate affairs. She took Blackie on a ride through the woods, and if she rode him particularly hard, the horse was the only one who noticed. She reread the recent letter from Margaret with considerable less patience than when she had perused it a few days earlier. Margaret advised her to choose the man with whom she could envision herself old and comfortable. She could imagine herself old with Geoffrey, but somehow she didn't think their lifestyle would be sedate enough to be comfortable. She rather thought he'd die on horseback, winning a race at age eighty-four. She could envision herself as an elderly marchioness, with the marquis still elegant with silver hair and an ebony cane. Still, that picture didn't bring her much comfort either. Lady Janice's suggestion seemed more and more like the answer to her problems, but she wasn't sure she had the courage to implement it.

The marquis was pleasant and polite at luncheon, making witty conversation that made her laugh and actually brought a smile to her mother's face. Watching the answering smile light his sapphire eyes and soften his usually firm mouth, she made her decision. He hadn't even left the room before she linked her arm in his.

The marquis looked down at her, eyebrow raised in obvious surprise.

"I believe you had expressed an interest in seeing how our rose gardens had handled the chill last night," she remarked for her mother's benefit. To Allison's surprise, her mother sailed from the room without so much as a backward glance. Allison couldn't help frowning at her retreating back. The widow Munroe was manipulating her again, she was sure of it. She just wasn't sure how. Beside her the marquis coughed politely to get her attention.

"You know how I value the beauty of roses," he replied when she met his gaze. She started, seeing the calculation written therein. Pasting on a polite smile, she led him out to the gardens.

They strolled among the bushes, although Allison scarcely noticed whether any of the many bright blooms had been blighted by the frost of the night before. She barely noticed that the air was a bit cool, chilling her through her blue sprigged-muslin gown, or that her flounced skirts swept aside the fall leaves as she wandered along the paths. She could not believe she was going to be so bold as to ask a gentleman to kiss her. She was mad, she must be, to even think of it. If he spoke of the matter to anyone, her reputation would suffer. Yet she had to know. She bit her lip and tried to think of a logical way to proceed. They were in the center of the circle of vibrant red blooms, their perfume heavy in the crisp fall air, when the marquis pulled her up short.

"All right, Miss Munroe," he said firmly, removing his navy-sleeved arm from her grip. "You've made it abundantly clear that you want a private word with me. What can I do for you?"

Allison decided there was no use being evasive. "Kiss me," she told him.

His eyebrows shot up so high she wondered they didn't fly off his noble forehead. "I beg your pardon?"

Allison wrung her hands, afraid someone would find them before she could persuade him. "I know this seems odd, but it is very important to me. I want you to kiss me, as if you really meant it."

"I assure you, Miss Munroe," he replied with a wry chuckle, "I never kiss a woman unless I *do* mean it."

"Oh." His reply shook her. "Well, I certainly wouldn't want you to break an ethical code or anything. However, I would be truly grateful if you could find it in your heart to try to kiss me."

He crossed his arms over his chest. "May I ask why, particularly since you've rejected my suit?"

"Must you ask?" she fretted. When he didn't waiver, she sighed. "Very well. Lady Janice and my sister seem convinced that the only way to tell if one loves a gentleman is how one reacts to his kiss. I'm not sure I believe their theory, but I cannot send you away in good conscience until I have tried it."

His face was so stiff she thought he must be biting the inside of his cheeks.

"You're laughing at me," she accused him.

He let the laugh burst out. She ought to be angry with him, but there was something so pleasant in the sound that she caught herself smiling.

"I do believe, my lord," she grinned, "that that's the first time I've ever heard you truly laugh."

"You may be right," he chuckled. "I'm sorry, my dear. I can tell this means a great deal to you. I'm simply not used to a woman asking me to kiss her in broad daylight."

"Is it better in the dark?" Allison frowned.

He started laughing again. "I refuse to answer that on the grounds that you will have to marry me."

"Well, I certainly don't want that!" Allison declared. She gazed up at him, wavering between frustration and amusement. "Is there no way you will kiss me then?"

He sobered, gazing down at her. The light in his eyes sent a tremor up her spine. "If you insist, Miss Munroe, I'll do my best. Come here."

Allison swallowed and stepped closer. She could hear her heart hammering in her chest. Sweat dampened the inside of her gloves. She tried to keep her gaze on his, but the blue of his eyes seemed to be deepening, warming. She swallowed again and looked away.

The marquis rested his hand on her shoulder, pulling her toward him ever so gently. Then he lowered his head, and she felt his breath brush her cheek. Allison jumped.

The marquis smiled, pulling her toward him once more. Before she could move away again, he pressed his lips to hers.

She wasn't sure what she had been expecting after Janice and her sister's stories. Some sort of searing heat, perhaps, or an explosion of sensation in the center of her being. At the very least, she had thought she might go weak at the knees. Instead, the tingle of excitement she had felt faded. The kiss was pleasant; she'd give him that. His touch was gentle; his lips were warm. She could smell the bay rum cologne he used, feel the smoothness of his well-shaven chin. She could feel any number of

sensations. None of them were magical. She broke the
kiss and opened her eyes.

He released her and gazed down at her, his own eyes
dark, his breath coming more rapidly than she had
heard since the day he had raced her down the drive.
"Well?"

She smiled politely, mind whirling. "Thank you, my
lord. That was very instructive."

"Instructive, eh?" He stepped away from her, turning
to gaze at the roses. She knew he was trying to hide
the hurt, and she grit her teeth at her own ineptitude.
"Quite the blow to the ego, Miss Munroe," he murmured.

"I'm sorry," Allison offered lamely. "It was a very nice
kiss, my lord."

He barked out a laugh, and this time there was nothing happy about it. "Since we have just kissed, do you
think we might finally get beyond the Miss Munroe and
my lord stage?"

Allison felt herself blushing. "Of course, Thomas."
She considered asking whether he went by *Tom*, but she
doubted that sufficiently to make the asking not worth
the while.

"Thank you, Allison." He nodded. "I take it your curiosity is satisfied?"

"Yes, thank you," she replied, wishing she knew what
else to say to him. The kiss had obviously affected him
more than it had her, and she felt truly sorry that she
had not reciprocated. Then a chilling thought hit: What
if she couldn't reciprocate? She was the child of a
woman who prided herself on her cool reception to
matters of emotion. Could she, deep down, be as cool
as her mother? What if she never caught the fire of
passion?

The marquis offered her a bow. "Then I think perhaps I should take my leave for now. Your servant, Miss Allison."

She nodded absently, chewing her lower lip. She had called the kiss instructive, and now she knew the words had been well-chosen. It had given her much to think about. She simply wasn't sure what she was supposed to do for answers.

Seventeen

Geoffrey strained to see over Enoch's dark head as another carriage pulled up before the manor.

"It isn't them," Enoch grumbled, taking a swig of the scrumpy Henry Jarvis had contributed to the Guy Fawkes Day celebration. He grimaced as the hard Somerset cider burned a familiar path down his insides. "If you ask me, we've done all this work for nothing."

"They'll be here," Geoffrey maintained. "Genevieve promised." He glanced across the bonfire, already sending flames over five feet high, to the terrace of the manor, where his sister-in-law sat draped in furs to ward off the night chill. He knew the pile of furs in the high-backed chair next to hers was his mother. Beside them, Alan wrapped his greatcoat and muffler a little tighter about his throat. They'd have been warmer closer to the fire, but Alan was afraid of Gen getting too warm and Gen wanted nothing to do with Enoch.

"You sure you want to do this?" Enoch probed, stomping his booted feet as if to work the blood down to them. "Might make yourself a powerful enemy."

Geoffrey shook his head. "I don't care what the marquis thinks of me. Allison is all that matters."

"And you think this will win her?" Enoch's voice was sarcastic, and Geoffrey glanced his way. The man's blue eyes were sharp and bright over his open tweed greatcoat, and the light had nothing to do with the scrumpy they had both been drinking.

"Genevieve said Allison turned the marquis down," he told his mentor firmly. "But she has yet to announce it publicly. I haven't seen him posting off for London in the last three days. And the one time I was allowed to call with Genevieve, Allison barely spoke to me. It's clear he still has some hold on her. I mean to break it."

Enoch snorted. "And break your own neck in the process. Just tell the girl you love her and have done with it."

"It isn't enough that I tell her," Geoffrey replied heatedly, shrugging out of his own greatcoat. "I have to show her."

"By showing up the marquis?" Enoch took another swig of the cider. "I'll say this again, boy: You'd do better to simply ride up on Samson and kidnap the girl for Gretna."

Geoffrey made a face. "That's what I've been wanting to do since this all started. This time, I do things my way." He brightened. "Besides, my magnanimous sister-in-law suggested I act like a Pentercast."

"I think she was thinking of your brother," Enoch warned. "Not your father. Too many people still remember the time he set fire to the fields before the hay was in."

"I'm not drunk, if that's what you're afraid of," Geoffrey countered, the fire still too warm for his tweed coat and trousers. "I learned my lesson last Christmas. My head is clear. There will be no fields burned, but I won't make the same promise about other things."

Enoch shook his head and muttered into his tankard of cider.

By the time the Munroes arrived, nearly the entire village of Wenwood had gathered around the bonfire at the back of the manor. The multi-paned windows of the three-story block of a house leapt with reflections of the glowing flames. A long trestle table had been set up on the terrace, and neighbors were helping themselves of the bounty each had brought to share. Scrumpy, whiskey, ale, and cider passed from hand to hand. Someone began singing the carol of Guy Fawkes and others took up the chorus:

> Please to remember
> The fifth of November
> Gunpowder, treason and plot
> I see no reason
> Why gunpowder treason
> Should ever be forgot.

Geoffrey looked up from the last words to find Allison eyeing him around the curve of the fire. She was wearing a dove-gray fur-trimmed cloak, the hood thrown back to show flaxen curls framing her face as they escaped the bun behind her. In the light of the fire, her eyes shone a deep blue. Geoffrey raised his tankard to her in salute.

She leaned over to her mother and pointed to where her sister sat on the terrace. Her mother moved in that direction. The Marquis DeGuis stepped into the space she had vacated. Geoffrey's smile faded.

Allison turned to the marquis and smiled. "I don't remember celebrating Guy Fawkes Day in London when I lived there while Gen was going to finishing school. Do Londoners have bonfires such as this?"

"Not so near the houses," he replied, taking a cautious sip of the tankard he had been handed shortly after they arrived. He rolled the scrumpy around on his tongue, and his eyes widened. Allison tried not to smile as he set the tankard hastily down.

"Was I supposed to drink that or light the lamp with it?" he managed.

"Our cider has its own teeth," Geoffrey replied for her, materializing out of the darkness at her other side. Allison jumped, then scolded herself for feeling guilty. Geoffrey offered her a cup of the softer cider.

Allison took it gladly. "What a lovely fire, Geoffrey. You and the village lads must have been begging for coals all day."

"I remember doing that when I was a lad," the marquis mused. The insult was subtle, not unlike the man who had made it, but Geoffrey caught the innuendo. Allison did not.

"Then you did celebrate Guy Fawkes Day," she said encouragingly. "What kinds of parties did you have?"

"Nothing of much interest that I can recall," he replied. "On one of my estates in the North, however, they have a custom the eve of Guy Fawkes called *mischief night*. They play all kinds of pranks on their neighbors. I'm sure Mr. Pentercast would feel right at home."

Another insult. Geoffrey turned away to hide his smile. If the man only knew how easy he was making Geoffrey feel about his plans. Allison grinned, nudging him. "I wager you would like that, Geoffrey. Who are we burning tonight?"

Geoffrey started, frowning at her. But her smile was bright and she gave no indication she had any idea what he was planning. "Napoleon, of course, moonling. Who else has been vile enough to warrant such treatment?"

He met the marquis's eye and smiled. The marquis's eyes narrowed.

"Excellent choice," Allison concurred, saluting him with her cup of cider. She took a sip, then lowered it, watching him. She must have been getting awfully good at these social games, for she was certain Geoffrey hadn't noticed anything unusual about her. Once again, her heart was hammering against her rib cage and she could barely hold the cup of cider without spilling it in her trembling. She had decided that, tonight, she was going to have Geoffrey kiss her.

It was much easier than she thought to get him away from the bonfire. Even eight feet away the night closed in and the feeling of privacy was evident. "Mother brought some of Annie's pies for the feast," she told Geoffrey. "Be a dear, Geoffrey, and go fetch them from the carriage."

Geoffrey's eyes narrowed and she thought for a moment he would remind her that there were servants to take care of that sort of thing. Then he shrugged and went to do as she bid. She smiled pleasantly at the marquis, telling her rampaging heart to slow down, all the while watching to see when Geoffrey returned. When she made him out on the lantern-lit terrace, she sighed and handed her cider to the surprised Marquis.

"That man never can get anything right. He has put them in with the hams of all things. No one will find them there. Excuse me, Thomas. I'll be back in a moment."

She met Geoffrey at the foot of the stairs and drew him into the pool of darkness at the back of the house.

"Now what?" he growled.

She had rehearsed her speech this time. "Geoffrey, you have been asking me for some time to consider your suit. I am ready to do so."

Geoffrey peered at her in the darkness, sure he must have misheard. Perhaps he had taken one too many sips of the scrumpy, after all. "I don't understand," he murmured.

Allison took a deep breath. "I have been told that the only way to be certain one loves a gentleman is to kiss him. I tried it with the marquis."

"What!" Geoffrey shouted.

"Hush!" Allison cried, grabbing his arm and dragging him farther away from the fire and the crowd. "Listen to me, if you please. I'm trying to tell you something important."

"If you mean to tell me you've decided to marry him, after all, you may save your breath," he declared, shaken. "Damnation, Allison, how could you? Was one kiss so powerful that you are ready to give yourself to the man?"

"No." she declared. "His kiss was mediocre at best."

He felt an absurd grin replacing his frown. "Mediocre?"

"Don't be smug," she replied, wrinkling her nose. "It made me think, Geoffrey. Everyone says kisses are so important, yet his kiss made me feel nothing. I thought perhaps it simply meant I did not love him, but then I began to wonder." She swallowed and lowered her voice, almost afraid to say the words aloud. "What if I'm like Mother, Geoffrey? What if I'll never feel passionate about any man?"

"Don't be absurd," Geoffrey scoffed, even though the same thought had crossed his mind the night of the ball. "You're one of the most spirited people I know, Allison. As I told you before, sometimes love comes quickly and other times it comes like a thief in the night. When you love someone, you'll know it, in the kiss and in other ways as well."

"How can you be so sure?" she countered, afraid to hope. "What if I react the same way to every kiss I ever have?"

"There's only one way to find out," Geoffrey replied. He pulled her into his arms and kissed her.

Allison went rigid. She had been prepared to ask to be kissed, but not to have a kiss taken from her. But her frozen state quickly thawed as the warmth of his kiss invaded her senses. Like the man himself, Geoffrey's

kiss was brash, demanding, fiery. It called an answering
heat from the center of her being throughout her entire
body. She threw her arms around him and threw herself
into the kiss, pressing herself against him, wrapping her
arms about his powerful frame. Geoffrey crushed her to
him, enveloped her in his arms, prolonging the kiss until she was breathless. Her knees weakened, and she
heard the sound of a mighty explosion. The night
brightened around her in gold and silver. She let go of
him, stunned, and opened her eyes.

There was another explosion as the second mortar
went off. With a shower of sparks, the second firework
lit the night sky.

Geoffrey grinned at her in its light. "Well?"

"Oh, Geoffrey," was all she could seem to get out.

His grin deepened and he pulled her to him again.

When at last he released her, he kept her close and
gazed down at her. She could see he was as shaken as
she was. "Marry me, Allison," he demanded, although
his voice trembled.

"Oh, Geoffrey," she said again, then unaccountably,
she felt a giggle building. "It appears you've kissed me
insensible."

"At least you know you can enjoy a kiss," he countered. "Now, answer the question. Will you marry me?"

Another firework went off, brightening the night with
crimson and emerald. Around the fire someone began
chanting. With cries of "Guy Fawkes" and "Bring on
the villain," two chairs began wending their way through
the crowd on the shoulders of the brawniest of the Wenwood men. From the safety of Geoffrey's arms, Allison
watched the procession. With the tricorn hat and frog-
ged coat, she was sure the first was Napoleon. The second could only be Guy Fawkes. But there was something
familiar about the navy coat and fawn trousers, the
shock of black hair someone had painted on the turnip

head, the haughty expression, and the perfectly tied, pristine cravat.

Allison turned wide eyes to Geoffrey, who had the audacity to grin. "Geoffrey Pentercast, you didn't!"

"What?" he asked innocently.

Allison withdrew from his embrace, disappointment keen. "Geoffrey, you told everyone you'd changed. You promised! How could you be so cruel?"

"Cruel!" he yelped. "Who's talking about cruel, Miss Keep-Every-Suitor-Dangling-As-Long-As-Possible? Do you think it kind to keep the marquis and I in suspense while you kiss us and push us away?"

"Oh!" Allison cried, stung. "You make it sound as if I were some kind of tease."

"Well, aren't you?"

"No." She could feel tears coming to her eyes and turned away, furious at him for not understanding her dilemma. Unfortunately, turning her back on Geoffrey only gave her a better view of the mock-marquis, now burning merrily in effigy while the villagers sang odes to it. "Geoffrey Pentercast, you are impossible. I wouldn't marry you if you were the last man alive!"

Eighteen

Geoffrey tried to apologize the next day. It was a half-hearted job, done mostly because Genevieve threatened to send him back to Enoch's to live permanently if he didn't try. Allison refused to see him, Mrs. Munroe didn't even bother sending a reply to his card, Chimes was nowhere to be found, and Perkins informed him haughtily that the Marquis DeGuis was making preparations to leave that day and could not be disturbed. It was just as well, Geoffrey thought as he turned toward home. He really had rather enjoyed the way the old fellow had gone up in flames. He couldn't truthfully say he was sorry about that.

He hadn't even made it out of the Abbey clearing when he was pulled up short by a hail. Turning, he saw the Marquis DeGuis striding toward him. His first inclination was to put his hands on either side of his head and stick out his tongue at the fellow. However, as that would hardly endear him to his brother's wife should she ever hear of it, he ignored the urge and waited for the man to meet him.

"Were you looking for me?" the marquis asked when they were side by side.

Geoffrey nodded. "Yes. I came to apologize. It appears some felt my jest last night was in poor taste." There, he had said it without actually debasing himself.

"Some people do not appreciate a sense of humor," the marquis replied calmly. "No harm done."

Geoffrey eyed him, noting the cool exterior, the reflective blue of his eyes. "You are too kind, my lord," he managed truthfully.

"Are you by any chance walking back to the manor?" the marquis asked, surprising him.

Geoffrey nodded. "Yes, I'm returning home."

"Might I walk with you? I'd like to take my leave from your brother and his wife. I'm returning to London today."

What harm could it do, Geoffrey thought. "Very well."

They fell into step beside each other, moving along the footpath that cut through the woods and would allow them to reach the manor in much less time than the long winding road.

"You knew I was leaving, I take it?" the marquis asked.

"Yes, Perkins mentioned it."

"And I believe you know why." He sighed. "Miss Munroe will not have me. An impressive young lady, that one. But then, I suppose I needn't tell you that."

"No," Geoffrey replied, belligerence building despite himself. "You needn't."

As if he sensed Geoffrey's mood, the marquis was silent for a time. The dry fall leaves crackled beneath their boots. A bird called away in the wood. Closer at hand, something rustled in the undergrowth.

"You haven't won, you know," the marquis murmured.

Geoffrey swung on him, halting. "You needn't tell me that either. In fact, you needn't tell me anything at all. You tried to marry the only girl I've ever wanted, despite the fact that you knew I wanted her and that she didn't want you. Don't try to be friendly now."

The marquis sighed. "I'm sorry, Pentercast. This isn't

easy for me either. Do you think I relish losing? Do you think I offer for every lovely young lady who happens on the marriage mart? I loved her, too, you know."

"No." Geoffrey scowled at him. "I didn't know."

He sighed again. "I haven't your flair for exposing my feelings. Miss Munroe embodies everything I desire in a wife." He stopped himself, then laughed sarcastically. "Miss Munroe. After all this time, you'd think I'd have gotten to the point where I could call her *Allison.* You beat me there as well."

"I've known Allison all her life," Geoffrey replied, hating himself for pitying the fellow. "We grew up together. It would be a little odd for me to start calling her *Miss Munroe* now, although I did try when I was working to show you up."

"Didn't have to work very hard, did you?" the marquis scoffed self-derisively. "I'm a poor excuse for a lover. Do you know, the only time I kissed her, she had to ask me to do it?"

"Good God, man," Geoffrey exclaimed, "don't you have any blood in those veins?"

" 'If you prick us, do we not bleed?' " he quoted from the Bard. "Perhaps my blood isn't quite as fiery as yours. My one consolation is that you'll make her a horrid husband."

"Watch it," Geoffrey growled, "or peer or no peer, you'll meet my fists."

The marquis shook his head. "That would serve little purpose now, don't you think?"

"It might make me feel a great deal better," Geoffrey replied, tempted beyond anything.

The marquis stopped, again eyeing him. "You want to fight? I warn you, I was taught by Gentleman Jackson himself."

"And I was taught by three of Wenwood's finest bullies," Geoffrey replied. He peeled off his tweed coat and began rolling up the sleeves of his lawn shirt. "What do you say, my lord? A bare-knuckles brawl, out here, where no one can see us."

The marquis peeled off his own fine woolen coat and rolled up the sleeves of his silk shirt. "No one to witness your crushing defeat."

"No one to impress," Geoffrey countered, raising his fists.

"No one to stop us," the marquis agreed, raising his own.

They faced off on either side of the footpath, trees at their backs and leaves underfoot. The wood had gone silent. The marquis circled to the right. Geoffrey swung in, and he deftly blocked it. Geoffrey pulled back, surprised by the strength of the move. The marquis kept circling.

Geoffrey tried another roundhouse swing, only to find that the marquis was ready for him. Not only ready, but the man had obviously taken his measure. He blocked with his left and jabbed Geoffrey hard on the chin with his right. Pain shot up his jaw, and instead of stepping back, he stumbled. The marquis closed, but Geoffrey managed to turn under the blow. Straightening, he widened the distance between them.

"You'll never win that way, Pentercast," the marquis called. "My reach is as long as yours; neither of us can get a blow in this way."

"I wouldn't bet on that," Geoffrey replied. He burst out of his half crouch and slammed his fist toward the marquis nose. Again the man's hand blocked him easily, and again Geoffrey felt the sting of another hit, this time in the mouth. He fell back and licked the blood from his split lip.

"You can see our differences rather clearly this way," the marquis panted, returning to his circling move. "You fight full of passion and headless enthusiasm. I consider the impact of my blows before delivering them."

"You keep a cool head," Geoffrey allowed, determined not to be hit again. "Most people would call that an admirable quality."

"But you don't," the marquis taunted.

"I," Geoffrey replied, dropping his guard only slightly and watching him, "am not most people."

The marquis couldn't pass up an easy opening, just as Geoffrey had hoped. His upper cut whizzed within inches of Geoffrey's nose, the breeze fanning his cheeks. Geoffrey rushed in under the arm, grabbing him in a bear hug and crushing his ribs. The marquis brought an elbow down between his shoulder blades, but Geoffrey hung on and squeezed. Then he tightened his leg muscles, strained his back, and heaved the marquis up and off his feet. Geoffrey hurled him back into a tree and watched in satisfaction as he slid to the ground at its base.

He wiped the blood off his lip with the back of his hand and waited for the marquis to rise. Instead, the man only regarded him.

"I repeat," he said, breath coming in gulps, "you'll make her a horrid husband. I stand by my words."

"Stand?" Geoffrey scoffed. "You can't even get up. Admit it, my fine Marquis. I've beaten you."

The marquis pushed himself to his feet, wincing, and attempted to straighten. He teetered, but only got halfway up before he cringed, clutching his ribs, and stopped. "Yes, you've beaten me. But you haven't won. Don't you see, Pentercast? You're a sham of a gentleman. Miss Munroe may be fooled, but I'm not. You're an animal, an ogre. You're not fit to be found in polite society, and you're certainly not good enough to marry a wonderful woman like Allison Munroe."

"Enough!" Geoffrey shouted at him, maddened beyond all reason. "One more word, and so help me, I'll flatten you again!"

The marquis shook his head. "You can flatten me as much as you like. It won't change the facts. If you were any kind of man, you'd let her find some other fellow to wed. You'd do the honorable thing and walk away."

"I said *enough.*"

"You claim to love her," the marquis continued, each word a nail in his heart, "but you expect her to stay tied to you in this miserable little backwater in some hovel you'll build. What will you do, Geoffrey, when she realizes what she's given up for you? Or do you plan to keep her breeding so she's too busy taking care of a pack of animals like their father to wonder what brought her to this pass? Or are you going to knock her off her feet as well?"

"Get up," Geoffrey snarled, bending to retrieve his coat and throwing it at him. "Get up and get out of Wenwood. If I ever see you here again, I'll . . ."

"Yes, I know," the marquis replied dryly, struggling to his feet. "You'll knock me down again. How very original. Goodbye, Pentercast. Try to find some place in that primitive brain of yours to think about what I've said. Allison is too fine a woman to be saddled with the likes of you." He managed to limp back down the path toward the Abbey.

Geoffrey watched him go, chest heaving. The sheer arrogance of the man! It could only be envy talking. Geoffrey still had a chance to win Allison, where the marquis had destroyed his. He ought to pity the man.

But as he picked up his own coat and started once more for home, the words seemed to hang in the air around him. He was a bear of a man, everyone from his family to the village lads in Wenwood to the few citizens of London he had met would agree with that. He was tough and gruff and had far too many rough

edges to play the polished Corinthian for long. Truth
be told, he had always rather prided himself on the fact
that he didn't put on airs above his station. He was the
second son of a country squire. If Alan hadn't been
such a caring brother, he would have been canyon fod-
der for Wellington's army long since.

He'd tried to polish himself to win Allison, of course.
And he thought he had made a credible Society gentleman, at least for a short time. He hadn't thought Allison
had enjoyed playing the Society belle. She seemed much
more at ease here in the country. But she did deserve
better, a part of him argued. DeGuis was right when he
had said she was a fine woman. Geoffrey had never met
her match. There wasn't a woman in Wenwood or the
surrounding countryside who could dance and ride and
laugh as well as Allison Munroe. And while some might
have a greater claim to beauty, none of them moved
him as she did. But there he was, thinking about his
own wants and needs again. What of Allison's?

Would she be better off if he gave up his suit? There
had been other lads at the Barnsley Assembly who
would have been only to glad to court her, if they had
been as sure that she wasn't already taken with the marquis. If Chas Prestwick hadn't repaired to London, he
would have probably been after her. Of course, he was
only a second son as well, but the second son of an
earl was far more impressive than a second son of a
squire. Tom Harvey had been smiling at her for years,
but she'd never noticed. No, Allison would have no lack
of suitors once word got out that she was available
again.

Which meant that if he wanted to keep her, he had
to act quickly. But should he act at all? She had yet to
claim she loved him, their tremendous kiss notwithstand-
ing. Instead of hounding her as the marquis had done,
perhaps it was the best thing for everyone if he simply

let nature take its course. Perhaps the best thing was to give Allison some time to think.

Only he was afraid that if he thought much more, he would end up doing exactly as the marquis had suggested and walk away forever.

Nineteen

"Turned you down, did she?" Enoch growled, dabbing his lip with witch hazel.

Geoffrey grimaced at the pain the man's touch brought. "Yes," he mumbled through the ministrations, glad that the grooms were out in the fields with the horses that afternoon. He didn't much need additional eyes to witness his misery. "I guess you can say that I got both my lip and my heart bloodied."

"Witch hazel only works on lips," Enoch replied, tossing the piece of cloth he had been using into a dustbin at the side of the great oak worktable. "So, what now?"

Geoffrey shook his head. "I don't know. The marquis said I should do the honorable thing and let her go."

"What do you think?" Enoch asked him, sharp eyes narrowed.

"I don't know," Geoffrey repeated, wriggling on the hard wood stool under the man's continued stare.

Enoch dusted off his hands on his tattered tweed work clothes. "Well, you're not a great deal of use today, are you now? Perhaps the marquis was right—you don't deserve a lovely young lady like Miss Allison."

Geoffrey closed his eyes, trying to ignore the throb from his lip. "You don't have to confirm it."

"Then again," Enoch continued thoughtfully, "there's those who say that Miss Allison brought all this on her own head. Those Munroe women have always been a bit on the wayward side."

"Don't start," Geoffrey growled, eyes snapping open. "I said as much last night, and I've been regretting it since. It isn't Allison's behavior that's lacking; it's my own."

Enoch cocked his head. "Sure of that, are you? Seems to me that she's kept the two of you caged all Season, like the pet ferret she keeps."

"I gave her that ferret," Geoffrey informed him testily. "It wouldn't be in a cage but for me." He stopped for a moment, staring at Enoch. "And I wouldn't be either! Nor would the marquis, if we'd have had the good sense to get ourselves out."

"Now what are you nattering on about?" Enoch grumbled.

Geoffrey was too excited to let the matter go, hopping off the stool to pace about the straw-strewn plank flooring. "Don't you see, Enoch? The marquis and I both put ourselves in cages, and we've been trying to get out of them all Season. The marquis locked himself in when he tried to get Allison's hand without going to her first. That fact cost him her respect. He's been trying to get out ever since."

"I'll give you it was a mistake not to go straight to the girl," Enoch allowed. "But what about you?"

"I was even more blind. I locked myself in when I agreed to try to be something I'm not. I spent all Season trying to please my family, Allison's family, even the marquis! I was so proud of how I'd changed. I never really thought about just being myself."

"Thought that's what you did last night," Enoch muttered.

Geoffrey hung his head. "I suppose I did. But that was a mistake as well. You once asked me what Alan expected me to learn from my time with you. I think I finally understand what that is. If I'd seen it sooner, I might have been married to Allison by now. It is so simple: Being myself is no excuse for being less to others." He reached for his greatcoat, thrown hurriedly over one of the other stools at the worktable. "Thank you, Enoch, for all you've taught me. I know what I have to do now. Wish me luck."

"I'd be happy to," the man growled, eyeing him as he strode to the door, "if I knew what it was you were going to do."

"I'm going to do the thing I wanted to do all Season," Geoffrey declared. "I'm going to tell Allison Munroe I love her and ask her to marry me. And this time, I'm going to do it my way."

Allison wandered down the hall of the manor, ill at ease and at a loss for what to do next. Her mother and she had seen the marquis off only hours before. She was sure she had shocked them both when she had impulsively hugged the poor man. The grimace on his face as she pulled away had been evidence of that. But she was truly sorry things hadn't worked out differently. And she was still embarrassed for her family, and her village, that Geoffrey had gone so far as to burn the poor man in effigy last night.

She found herself in the music room and plunked herself down at the spinet, running a hand up the keys. The octave sounded sad to her. She let her hands fall to the sides of her green sprigged-muslin gown and sighed. First too many suitors and now not enough. Apparently she simply couldn't have things the way she wanted them.

And what did she want? Her hand drifted to her mouth as she remembered Geoffrey's kiss. The only word for it was *impressive*. If he'd have kissed Lady Janice like that, the girl would have defied her parents to marry him, Allison was sure. Why, half the unmarried ladies in Wenwood would have married him for such a kiss! And she had declared in ringing tones that nothing would prevail upon her to do so. She shook her head. How very foolish!

Did she love Geoffrey? Not for the first time did she wish her father were still alive. Rutherford Munroe had been a man who lived life to its fullest. He would have been able to advise her, she was sure, as to what her heart was trying to say to her. If only her mother were more approachable!

As if in answer to her thoughts, her mother moved into the room, Perkins at her heels like an elderly spaniel. She spied Allison at the spinet and paused. "Were you going to play, my dear?"

"No." Allison sighed, rising to make way for her mother. "Please play if you want to, Mother."

Her mother nodded, spreading her lavender skirts to sit on the bench. Her hands moved over the keys and a soft melody drifted from the instrument. Allison wandered over and sank onto the sofa. She tried to ignore Perkins at his post beside the door.

"You seem out of sorts today," her mother mused over the music. "Do you miss London?"

Allison shuddered. "No, I do not. I never thought I'd say this, Mother, but I quite prefer the country. If I never return to London, it will be too soon."

Her mother frowned, but Allison couldn't tell if she were trying to concentrate on the music before her or whether she disagreed with Allison's opinion. "Then you are determined to follow this course of becoming a governess."

"No, Mother." Allison smiled. "I only said that to prove to you how determined I am to make my own way. Not that I wouldn't go through with it," she hur-

ried on when her mother eyed her in a particularly
calculating manner. "It simply would not be my first
choice."

"Then you still believe in finding a husband," her
mother murmured, hope evident despite her calm demeanor.

"Yes, I do," Allison declared. "I only wish . . ."

"What?" her mother prompted.

Allison sighed. "I only wish I knew more about love."

"Perkins," the widow Munroe intoned, startling Allison with her sternness. "Please fetch us some tea." As
the butler bowed and made his slow way down the corridor, she nodded to her daughter. "Please continue,
Allison."

Allison struggled not to frown. Her mother was obviously trying to give them an opportunity to really talk
for a change. After recent events, she wasn't sure she
was willing to do so. She watched her mother for a moment, then decided that nothing ventured was nothing
gained. "Did you love Father, Mother?"

To her surprise, the sweetest of smiles spread on her
mother's face, turning the gray eyes to quicksilver and
making her look years younger. "Oh, yes, Allison. I
don't think it's possible I could have loved him more.
He was the most wonderful man in the world! He was
thoughtful; he was generous; he was kind. There wasn't
a person who didn't like him from the moment they
laid eyes on him. He had the uncanny knack of knowing
when to be silent in understanding and when to make
one laugh, even at oneself. I . . . I miss him terribly."
She stopped playing and hung her head, sniffing back
a sob.

Allison leapt from the sofa and ran to give her a
fierce hug. Her mother held her close, and Allison
could feel her shaking. "Oh, Mother, I'm so sorry," she

offered, ashamed not to have asked before. "I never knew. I wasn't even sure you liked him."

"Liking and loving are two different things," her mother sniffed, straightening to tug a handkerchief from her sleeve. "There were times when your father's behavior was not what I would have chosen. However, I always loved him." She dabbed at her eyes and Allison looked away, concerned she was making her mother feel self-conscious. When she was sure her mother had recovered, she couldn't help continuing the conversation.

"How did you know you loved him?"

Her mother looked thoughtful. "I think I knew it when I realized I was only truly alive when I was with him. He had a way of making me feel as if I were capable of anything. Nothing was ever too daunting or difficult for Rutherford. He had that kind of attitude that made you believe you could fly, if you wanted to."

Allison smiled. "I remember."

Her mother eyed her. "The marquis never made you feel that way, did he?"

"No." She shook her head. "I was never sure what to do or say around him. It was rather awkward, really. The only person besides Father who ever made me feel as if I could do no wrong is . . ." She stared at her mother and slowly rose to her feet.

"Geoffrey Pentercast," her mother finished for her, grimacing.

Allison nodded numbly. "Yes, how did you know?"

"You seem happier with him than with anyone," her mother replied with a sigh. "I had hoped it was only a momentary fancy, but I should have known better. It appears I shall have to have two Pentercast sons-in-law."

"But, Mother," Allison protested, feeling suddenly breathless, "we disagree so often. He can make me furious."

"Would you rather have a life with someone like the

marquis, who never made you feel anything at all?" her mother replied.

Allison shook her head, feeling a smile spreading. "No, never." She threw her arms about her mother and squeezed her tight. "Oh, Mother, thank you! You've no idea how much you've helped."

"I can be good for some things," her mother sniffed. "Now, if you please, you have delayed my practice long enough. I believe you have other things you wish to do."

Allison laughed, jumping to her feet. "Yes, thank you. I'm going riding."

"Try not to talk to Enoch McCreedy," her mother cautioned as she dashed for the door. "That man is the most uncivil person I know."

Allison grinned. "Yes, Mother. And if I do, I shall try to moderate my tone."

Allison changed into her blue velvet riding habit and had the groom saddle Blackie. How could she have been so blind? She had been so intent on looking for an overwhelming passion, she had disregarded the warmth and happiness she already had. In a sense, she supposed, both her cousin Margaret and Lady Janice were right. Love was bound up with friendship, admiration, and commonality of purpose; but it had a spark of something more. And she had found all those things in Geoffrey Pentercast. Why did she need to look any farther?

She was completely intent on riding down the drive and across the fields to Enoch McCreedy's farm, where she was sure she'd find Geoffrey this time of day. Unfortunately, she only made it to the bend in the drive that connected with the lane to the manor. Sitting squat in the way stood the brown-lacquered hulk of the Pentercast landau. The four matching bay horses fretted in the traces; the driver was no where in sight, and the attendant groom in his brown tweed jacket was peering into the open door of the carriage as if something or someone inside had captured all his attention.

"Ho, there," Allison called, pulling Blackie up short beside the equipage. "What is going on here?"

The groom jumped, pulling back and whirling to face her. His narrow face was ashen and she had never seen anyone's eyes so wide. "Miss Munroe, oh, Miss Munroe, what shall we do?" he gasped, wringing his hands. "I've never birthed a baby!"

"Baby!" Allison cried, staring at the carriage in horror.

"Allison?" Her sister's voice drifted tremulously out of the dark interior. "Is that you?"

"Yes, Gen," Allison called, motioning frantically to the groom to help her from the sidesaddle. It took several seconds for the man to understand what she was about; then he stood patiently while she slid down into his thin arms. He set her carefully on the ground. Allison snatched up the reins where he had let them fall and thrust them at him. "Here, take care of Blackie."

He nodded dully. Allison pushed past him to the carriage.

She peered inside, almost afraid of what she might see. Genevieve was leaning rather awkwardly back in the seat, her dark woolen skirts spread before her. They hung heavily against the floor as if they were sodden. Allison frowned, gazing up at her sister's face, a pale oval against the dark velvet upholstery.

Gen managed a strained smile. "Good afternoon, dearest. I think the baby is coming."

Allison felt as if someone had shoved a rock against her stomach. "Now?" she croaked.

Gen grimaced, and her hands gripped her belly. "Now!" she grunted.

"Oh my God," the groom muttered outside.

"Be silent!" Allison snapped at him. She clambered into the coach, rocking it, and Gen moaned. Gingerly, Allison took a seat beside her sister.

"What should I do?"

Gen gasped in a breath and relaxed against the squabs, eyeing Allison with surprising belligerence. "How am I supposed to know! This is my first baby!"

"But I thought all married ladies knew!" Allison cried, feeling the panic building. "Didn't Mother tell you? Didn't Dr. Praxton say anything?"

"As they assumed they would be there to assist, I doubt either thought it necessary," her sister replied crossly. She rubbed her abdomen softly. "I sent the coachman through the woods to the Abbey. Alan is in the village, and today is Mother Pentercast's day to visit the pensioners. She took the other carriage earlier this morning."

"He should have been back by now," the groom mumbled through the open door. He was trying to avert his eyes respectfully and his curiosity was getting the best of him. It only served to make him look slightly cross-eyed.

"Someone will come," Gen insisted. "Mother will know what to do, and so will Bryce. And they can send someone for Dr. Praxton."

"Do we have that much time?" Allison asked hesitantly, thinking how much territory the country doctor often covered. "He could be anywhere from Barnsley to Prestwick Park."

"Well, he can jolly well get here now," Gen snapped. Then she closed her eyes and stiffened, clutching her stomach. As Allison watched in horror, her face contorted and she cried out. Allison reached for her, only to draw back, unsure of what to do. The spasm only lasted a few seconds; then her sister collapsed back into a heap, gasping.

"Oh, Gen, that was awful!" Allison moaned.

"You may call it awful," Gen growled. "It isn't your belly a creature is trying to claw its way out of."

Allison felt herself blanch. "What, what can we do?"

"Well, we have to do something!" There was a manic note in her sister's voice, and her eyes gleamed with an unholy light that frightened Allison. "I can't do this alone. We have to find someone who knows about babies, and quickly."

"Ladies," a deep warm voice said from the side of the carriage. "Might I be of assistance?"

Allison stared at him, hope filling her.

Genevieve took one look at Geoffrey Pentercast, silhouetted in the door of the carriage with the sun a halo about his head, and fainted.

Twenty

Geoffrey had taken Samson and ridden straight for the Abbey. He had never felt so free, or so determined. His fate stood before him, and he knew it was up to him to seize it, or die trying. Like a cavalry officer facing Napoleon's canons, he narrowed his eyes and urged his mount forward.

He didn't falter when he found the door to the Abbey standing open. Striding in, fully intending on glaring Perkins down if necessary to find Allison, he was at last forced to pull up short by the scene before him. The manor's Coachman Jack was standing in the center of the parquet-floored entry, trembling and wringing his hands. The sight of the man who could calmly handle a coach-and-six through a crowded city street so discomposed shook Geoffrey. He frowned at Perkins, who was standing rigidly in front of the man, back straight, gaze implacable. Then he caught sight of Chimes, who was leaning against the far wall, watching the display in his shirtsleeves with what could only be called unholy glee. Geoffrey's eyes narrowed still further.

"What's going on here?" he demanded, breaking in between the city butler and the coachman. The burly Jack Coachman turned an anguished brown-eyed gaze on him.

"Master Geoffrey, thank God! Tell this idiot I must

speak to Mrs. Munroe right now. Mrs. Pentercast needs her!"

"Has something happened to my mother?" Geoffrey demanded with a frown.

The coachman shook his head. "Not the dowager Mrs. Pentercast, sir, the younger. She's having a baby."

Geoffrey felt as if he were having one himself by the grip that seized his gut. Perkins merely sniffed.

"As I explained to this gentleman, Mrs. Munroe is indisposed and cannot be disturbed. If Mrs. Pentercast has chosen to give birth prematurely, she will simply have to do it alone."

Geoffrey stared at him. "Are you mad? Send for Mrs. Munroe immediately, you idiot. Genevieve may have my mother with her, but she'll want her own mother as well."

"But that's just it, sir," Jack Coachman protested, shaking so hard that he knocked the battered top hat from his graying head. "She doesn't have her mother with her. She isn't even at the manor! She's in the landau halfway between here and the manor, with only young Peter at her side."

"What!" Geoffrey yelped, mind churning with his gut. Abandoning any hope of moving the overfastidious butler, he strode to Chimes's side. "Did you hear that? How can you stand there and listen to this idiot? Get Mrs. Munroe and quickly."

Chimes grinned at him. "I sent Mary for her ten minutes ago. With any luck, she's already being loaded into the carriage and on her way. I simply wanted to see how far his nibs would go in refusing."

"Thank you, Chimes." Geoffrey nodded, taking a deep breath to try to calm himself. "Did Miss Allison go with her?"

Chimes shook his head. "She left sometime earlier.

On her way to Enoch McCreedy's, I understand. Now, why do you suppose that might be?"

Despite his tension, Geoffrey caught himself grinning as well. "I could suppose a lot of things, but perhaps I'd better find out the truth by asking Allison. But first, I'm going to make sure Genevieve is all right."

He started to turn back to where Perkins and Jack Coachman stood locked in battle, but Chimes caught his arm. "Stop by here before you go home," he advised. "I'll have an overnight bag packed, just in case."

Geoffrey clapped him on the shoulder. "Chimes, you're a man after my own heart!"

He swept back through the entryway, grabbing the distraught coachman's arm as he did so and hauling him out of the Abbey. Perkins he left to Chimes's not-so-tender mercy. He quickly explained the situation to the coachman, who sagged in relief, then sent the man back through the woods to the manor so that the servants there could be ready. Then he sprang up onto Samson and galloped off down the drive.

As soon as he was around the bend that joined the Abbey drive with the one to the manor, he saw the carriage, with Blackie standing beside it. Now he gazed into the coach, amazed at the sight that met his eyes. Genevieve lay in a sodden heap against the worn velvet seat; the woman he loved was gazing at him in a most besotted manner that only made him want to leap over there and kiss her equally senseless, and he was pretty sure he had just volunteered himself to deliver his brother's child.

"Oh, Geoffrey," Allison cried, holding out her hands. "I'm so glad you're here!"

That was all the encouragement he needed to clamber up into the carriage. The motion was enough to rouse Gen, who eyed him dubiously as he settled himself on the seat opposite her.

"You," she said quellingly, "are not touching me."

"Now, Genevieve," he murmured soothingly, winking at the wide-eyed Allison. "I'll have you know I've delivered a baby before."

"When?" Gen demanded, eyes fiery. "Where?"

"This is not the time or place to discuss it," he replied, hoping he would not have to admit it had been a baby horse. "Besides, I've been to the Abbey. Your mother is on her way, and Jack Coachman is heading for the manor to get additional help. I only have to keep you company until they arrive."

"Oh, very well," Gen grumbled with a noted lack of graciousness. "Just keep that oaf of a groom away from me."

"As you please, mum." The groom scampered out of sight with obvious relief.

Allison watched Geoffrey, pride swelling, as he continued to talk in a calm, reasonable manner to her nearly hysterical sister. His large hands gently moved her into a more comfortable position before she even realized he was touching her as she had forbidden. His dark hair was tousled, his knotted cravat wrinkled beyond repair. He quickly abandoned his jacket and rolled up his sleeves. She could see the play of muscle in his arm as he urged her sister to lean farther back. Anyone seeing him now, she thought, would think him the gentlest man alive.

Geoffrey caught her watching him and winked at her again. He liked the way it brought a flush of pink to her cheeks. Beside him, Genevieve groaned again, writhing into a ball, and his attention was forced back to the matter at hand. He reached out to help, and she swatted his hand away. Rocking back, he motioned to Allison, who leaned toward him.

"It will help if you can keep her from straining so,"

he murmured. "Rub her back in a circular motion. Speak calmly to her."

Allison swallowed, eyeing her sister, who was panting and clutching her stomach. She was almost afraid to touch Gen in case she made the pain worse. "I'll try." She moved closer to her sister and began rubbing in circles. Gen glared at her, then shrugged her shoulders and rolled her neck as the rhythm helped relax her obviously tired muscles. Slowly she uncurled with a long, heartfelt sigh. Allison beamed at Geoffrey.

"That's better now," Geoffrey murmured, wondering how best to broach the next subject. If he were any judge by how quickly and hard the pains seemed to be coming, the baby would be bursting into sight any minute. He wasn't sure Genevieve was ready to raise her skirts in front of him, but he knew she could never birth the child without doing so.

Allison was thinking the same thing. Her father had taken her to see a lamb born once at the Pentercast barn. She was pretty sure a baby was born in much the same manner. Surely her sister would need to clear a path through the skirts and petticoats. As Gen closed her eyes for a moment, Allison motioned Geoffrey closer.

"You're wonderful," he murmured before she could speak. "Can you continue that rubbing awhile longer?"

She blushed under his praise. "As long as need be. But, Geoffrey, if it actually comes down to the baby being born, don't we have to raise her skirts?"

He nodded. "I have been thinking the same thing. I cannot do it, Allison. Genevieve would be mortified, and I'm not sure how Alan would feel about it, even given these circumstances. If I step outside, can you handle this alone?"

Allison grabbed his hand, feeling the panic rising again. "You'd leave me?"

"Never," he swore, holding her hand tightly. "I'd just be out of sight. If I'm right, it won't be for long."

Allison bit her lip. She glanced at her sister, who was even now twitching as the next birth pain began. "All right," she gasped. "But you'll talk to me? You'll explain what I should do?"

Geoffrey nodded. "Whatever you need. Quickly now. She's stirring." He slipped out of the carriage and shut the door.

Allison gazed down at her sister, curling into a ball now as the pain wracked her body. She moved closer, lifting the sodden skirts. As she had suspected, they were soaked with fluid and cold. "These cannot be helping," she murmured as Gen collapsed again. "Let's get these damp things out of the way, shall we?"

"Where's Geoffrey?" Gen demanded, rousing herself to gaze wildly about the coach.

"Just outside," Allison replied calmly, wrestling with her sister's clothing. "He'll come if we call, but he thought you might like some privacy."

Gen yawned, obviously exhausted. "About time," she muttered, submitting to Allison's tugging. To Allison's relief, she found that her sister was wearing divided drawers, with plenty of room for the baby to drop in the center. They managed to tuck the dress and petticoats up about her waist between pains.

"Is everything all right in there?" Geoffrey called, concerned by the rocking of the carriage.

"Fine," Allison replied. She dug under the seat of the carriage, thankful that someone had remembered to throw in some woolen lap robes. She spread these over her sister's legs. Gen smiled wanly. A moment later, and she convulsed again.

"The pains are coming awfully close together," she called out to Geoffrey, her brow knit in concern.

"That means the baby will be here soon," Geoffrey

called back, leaning against the sun-warmed wood. "Get your sister to lean back and encourage her to help the baby come."

Allison eyed her sister, who glared back at her. "How do we encourage the baby?" she asked.

"Tell your sister to push with her belly muscles. She must push the baby out."

Gen frowned, but before she could protest, another pain seized her and she was too busy combating it.

"I don't think she can with all the pain," Allison called back, worried by the sweat that stood out on Gen's brow.

"Use the pain," Geoffrey advised, trying to think how to tell a woman to do what he had seen the mare do naturally. "Push against it. It will help lessen it."

"Did you hear that?" Allison asked her sister as she lay panting in the aftermath.

Gen eyed her. "I heard. It sounds like so much nonsense. Only a man would think to fight against a birth pain. Oh!" Another pain wracked her; but this time, Allison saw she tried to do what Geoffrey had suggested. Gen's eyes widened.

"It works!"

Allison laughed in pure relief. "Wonderful. Keep doing it."

She took one of Gen's hands and squeezed each time a contraction hit. Gen pushed against the pain, holding her breath and gritting her teeth. Her face was fierce to behold. Geoffrey was right, Allison realized. It was rather like fighting a battle. She only hoped her sister would be victorious.

Geoffrey stood outside, listening to the grunts of pain and the cries of relief after each pain subsided. Soon now . . . it had to be soon. He wondered whether he would be this close when his own child came into the world. If he had anything to say about it, he'd be holding Allison in his arms. He rather pitied Alan for not being here to witness the birth.

He noticed the wide-eyed groom standing near the horses and sweating. Having pity on the man, he sent him ahead to the Abbey with the horses. He had no sooner done so then he heard the sound of approaching hoofbeats. His brother galloped up beside him, eyes wild.

"What's happened?" he demanded, leaping from the saddle. "I saw the coach halfway up the drive from the village."

Geoffrey caught his shoulder. Inside the coach, Genevieve cried out. Alan jerked away from him, pushing past him for the door.

"Easy," Geoffrey cautioned, catching him and holding him with difficulty. "The baby is nearly born. Go carefully, and you might just get to see it."

Alan stared at him, obviously shaken. "The baby. Here? Now? Where's Dr. Praxton?"

Geoffrey shrugged, stepping aside. "No one knows. But I doubt he'll get here in time. Allison is with her. Go ahead. She'll need your support."

Alan nodded blankly, fumbling with the door handle. Geoffrey helped him open it and averted his eyes as Alan climbed into the coach. Gen greeted him with a glad cry, and Allison moved aside to let him hold his wife in his arms. Smiling, Geoffrey shut the door.

He could hear Alan taking over, issuing gentle suggestions to both Allison and his wife. He knew his brother was the veteran of many nights in the lambing shed. Geoffrey closed his eyes and waited for the sound of the baby's arrival in the world. When the weak cry sounded, he was sure only the singing of angels could be sweeter.

It seemed only a short time later when the door opened again. He straightened, meeting Allison's glowing eyes. She broke his gaze to look down at the bundle in her arms. "Mr. Pentercast, I give you your niece, Allison Fancine Pentercast."

Geoffrey stared down at the tiny, red, wizened face nestled in the lap robe. Pride rose inside him. "They named her after you?"

"Well," Allison grinned at him, "it was a little hard to name her after you."

He laughed, running a hand back through his hair. "Yes, I suppose it was." He glanced up at Allison, noting how her ringlets were nearly flattened, hanging in lank ropes about her beaming face. Her riding habit was crushed and damp. Her face was streaked with dust and sweat. She had never looked lovelier. "Do you think I could hold her?" he asked.

Allison nodded, and he accepted the small body from her arms. The child nestled against him, offering him a yawn much like a kitten. Geoffrey stared at her, awed.

Allison climbed down beside him. He looked less rumpled than any of them, but that wasn't saying much. She could understand how her mother felt about her father. Standing before her was surely the most wonderful man in the world.

"I love you, Geoffrey," she murmured.

Geoffrey's head came up, the world suddenly spinning around him. He must be mad to think he had heard what he thought he had heard. "I . . . I beg your pardon?" he sputtered.

"Well," Allison grinned, "there have been a great many times when I think you should have begged my pardon, but when I have confessed that I love you isn't one of them. I do, you know. I'm sorry it's taken me so long to realize it."

Geoffrey blinked, took a step toward her, then belatedly realized he still held the baby. With a nervous laugh, he handed her back to Allison. Smiling, Allison accepted the baby and returned her to her joyous parents.

When she pulled back out of the carriage, she was surprised to find Geoffrey nowhere in sight. Craning her neck, she peered around the side of the carriage.

"Up here," Geoffrey called from the driver's box.

Allison frowned up at him. "What are you doing?"

"Do you think your sister can manage a short drive?" he asked. "I'd like to take us to the Abbey."

"I'll tell them." Allison nodded. She climbed back into the carriage not a little perplexed. Here she had just declared her love for the man, and he hadn't so much as acknowledged it! She crossed her arms on her chest and sat in the stuffy carriage while Alan and Genevieve billed and cooed over each other and their baby. By the time they had rattled their way up the drive to the Abbey, she had worked herself into quite a fit of pique.

The Munroe coachman was not as skilled as Jack Coachman in getting his horses harnessed and ready. Mrs. Munroe was still pacing in front of the stables, for once in her life actually looking a bit flustered, when Geoffrey drove the landau into the coaching yard. She was more than delighted to hustle the couple and the new grandchild into the Abbey in short order. Perkins seemed rather put out about the entire unorthodox state of affairs. Chimes merely winked at Geoffrey, throwing up a carpetbag that Geoffrey made fast to the luggage rack.

"Even her ladyship is put out with him this time," Chimes confided to Geoffrey gleefully. "I daresay he won't be with us much longer."

"Congratulations," Geoffrey replied with a smile.

"Congratulations yourself." Chimes chuckled. "I'm pleased to be able to say I said it before any of them.

I understand you can make Gretna by two days with a coach like this."

Geoffrey's smile widened.

Allison wandered toward the Abbey, feeling forgotten and abused. She was delighted for her sister and Alan, exhausted from the birth, and depressed beyond anything that Geoffrey hadn't cared enough to respond to her declaration. Her capricious behavior this Season had obviously destroyed any affection he had felt for her. Either that or he had simply run out of patience waiting for her love to bloom. Before she could let the tears she was holding back fall, Geoffrey caught her arm. "Oh, no, you don't," he declared, swinging her back toward him.

Allison grunted as she bumped against his solid chest. "What?" she snapped, hurt showing in her eyes, in the pout forming on her lips, and in the set of her shoulders. "Have you deigned to notice my existence at last?"

He grinned at her. "I've noticed your existence since you were born, moonling. I noticed it and I rather liked it. Now, I'm going to do what I should have done long months ago." He tightened his grip on her, and Allison's blood raced as she realized he was going to kiss her again. Before he could make good on the threat, however, he paused. "Do you want a huge wedding?"

"Wedding?" Allison squeaked. She threw her arms around him and hugged him. "Oh, Geoffrey, you do love me!"

He returned the hug, glorying in the feel of her. "Of course I love you, moonling. I may not have been able to say it, but I'm about to prove it."

"How?" Allison asked, pulling back, his tone sending shivers up her spine.

He kissed her once, sending fire throughout her chilled body, then twice, warming her to her toes, then a third time for good measure. "We're eloping to

Gretna Green," he murmured against her hair. "By the time anyone can protest, we'll be married."

"Oh, Geoffrey," Allison sighed. "Why didn't you think of that sooner?"

Epilogue

Wenwood, Somerset
Christmas Eve, 1813

Allison dangled the red ribbon in front of her name-sake's dear face and watched her dark-blue eyes widen.

"She looks just like Alan," the dowager Mrs. Pentercast proclaimed.

"My dear Fancine, you never could see what was in front of you," murmured Mrs. Munroe. "She clearly resembles Gen."

"You're both fair and far off," Geoffrey declared, climbing down from the ladder where he had been hanging the last of the kissing boughs in the Abbey withdrawing room. "If she looks like anyone, she looks like me."

The widow Munroe sniffed. Mrs. Pentercast smiled at him indulgently. Allison gazed at her husband thoughtfully.

"I do believe you are correct," she replied, trying to keep from grinning. "Her face is nearly as puckered as yours when you've come in from the winter cold after checking for the fourth time that those six percherons are all right. And there is a certain smell about her that reminds me of you, particularly when she needs changing."

Geoffrey scowled at her, and she gave it up and let

out a peal of laughter. Geoffrey held out his arms demandingly.

"I'll not have my niece influenced against me. Bring her here."

Still chuckling, Allison rose and did as he bid. He accepted the baby and darted in to kiss Allison on the cheek. When she started, he grinned, nodding up at the kissing bough overhead. Allison shook her head, smiling wryly.

Chimes pushed open the door to admit himself and Alan and Genevieve. Alan stomped his feet to ward off the winter chill and Genevieve hurried to take back her daughter. Chimes dragged the Yule log into the room and plopped it down next to the fireplace.

"And will you demand to be first to sit on it, Master Geoffrey, as you did last year?" he asked, dusting his hands off on his already rumpled black coat.

Geoffrey drew Allison into the circle of his arms. "Not I, Chimes. I have a fine house, the beginnings of a fine stable, and I'm married to the catch of the Season. I have all the luck I need."

Allison felt a warm glow and knew it wasn't the flames rising from the fire.

"Master Alan?" Chimes tried.

Alan pulled his wife and daughter close and shook his head. "Nor I. There's nothing I'd wish for I don't have right here."

Chimes glanced about the room. His black-eyed gaze fell on the widow Munroe. "Madame?"

Mrs. Munroe stiffened and merely glared at him. Mrs. Pentercast giggled. "No, thank you, Chimes, for both of us."

"What a pity," Mrs. Munroe murmured, snapping open her fan and applying it gently, "that Perkins did not work out. He seemed such a splendid butler."

"There she goes again," Chimes muttered, kicking

the log into the fireplace and heading toward the door. "As if that man would stay where there were likely to be children. No sense of family that one." He paused and rubbed his hands together, glancing over at Allison and Geoffrey. "You wait—your turn will be next. I feel it in my bones."

Allison blushed under the knowing black eyes. She glanced up at Geoffrey, who was grinning at the old man, unaware. She cleared her throat. "Actually, I feel it in my bones as well. And elsewhere."

Geoffrey gazed down at her, grin fading and eyes widening as he took her meaning. "Are you saying—"

She hugged him close. "It's a good thing you've had so much practice at birthing babies, Geoffrey. You're going to be a father."

Geoffrey kissed her soundly, then beamed. "Allison, that's . . . that's famous!"

"And speaking of birthing babies," Genevieve put in when congratulations had been passed all about. "I never did hear where you got such experience, Geoffrey. I own you did a marvelous job with my Allison. When did you learn?"

Geoffrey's eyes twinkled. "Do you really want to know?"

"Yes," she declared.

"Yes, please," Allison agreed beside him.

"Then gather around the fire, and I'll tell you the story of how I was exiled to Enoch McCreedy's farm."

"A farm?" Gen asked, paling. "Does this have anything to do with animals?"

Geoffrey grinned at her. "No ferrets, I promise. But I won't make the claim about other animals."

ABOUT THE AUTHOR

Regina Lundgen lives with her family in Kennewick, WA, and is the author of three previous Zebra Regency romances: *The Unflappable Miss Fairchild, The Twelve Days of Christmas,* and *The Bluestocking On His Knee.* She is currently working on her fifth, *A Dangerous Dalliance,* which will be published in May, 2000. Regina lives to hear from readers, and you may write to her at P.O. Box 7162, Kennewick, WA 99336-0616. Please include a self-addressed stamped envelope if you wish a response.

<u>BOOK YOUR PLACE ON OUR WEBSITE</u>
<u>AND MAKE THE</u>
<u>READING CONNECTION!</u>

We've created a customized website just for our very special readers, where you can get the inside scoop on everything that's going on with Zebra, Pinnacle and Kensington books.

When you come online, you'll have the exciting opportunity to:

- View covers of upcoming books
- Read sample chapters
- Learn about our future publishing schedule (listed by publication month *and author*)
- Find out when your favorite authors will be visiting a city near you
- Search for and order backlist books from our online catalog
- Check out author bios and background information
- Send e-mail to your favorite authors
- Meet the Kensington staff online
- Join us in weekly chats with authors, readers and other guests
- Get writing guidelines
- AND MUCH MORE!

Visit our website at
http://www.zebrabooks.com

More Zebra Regency Romances

__A Noble Pursuit by Sara Blayne $4.99US/$6.50CAN
    0-8217-5756-3

__Crossed Quills by Carola Dunn $4.99US/$6.50CAN
    0-8217-6007-6

__A Poet's Kiss by Valerie King $4.99US/$6.50CAN
    0-8217-5789-X

__Exquisite by Joan Overfield $5.99US/$7.50CAN
    0-8217-5894-2

__The Reluctant Lord by Teresa Desjardien $4.99US/$6.50CAN
    0-8217-5646-X

__A Dangerous Affair by Mona Gedney $4.50US/$5.50CAN
    0-8217-5294-4

__Love's Masquerade by Violet Hamilton $4.99US/$6.50CAN
    0-8217-5409-2

__Rake's Gambit by Meg-Lynn Roberts $4.99US/$6.50CAN
    0-8217-5687-7

__Cupid's Challenge by Jeanne Savery $4.50US/$5.50CAN
    0-8217-5240-5

__A Deceptive Bequest by Olivia Sumner $4.50US/$5.50CAN
    0-8217-5380-0

__A Taste for Love by Donna Bell $4.99US/$6.50CAN
    0-8217-6104-8

Call toll free **1-888-345-BOOK** to order by phone or use this coupon to order by mail.

Name_____

Address_____

City _____ State _____Zip_____

Please send me the books I have checked above.

I am enclosing $_____

Plus postage and handling* $_____

Sales tax (in New York and Tennessee only) $_____

Total amount enclosed $_____

*Add $2.50 for the first book and $.50 for each additional book.

Send check or money order (no cash or CODs) to:

Kensington Publishing Corp., 850 Third Avenue, New York, NY 10022

Prices and Numbers subject to change without notice.

All orders subject to availability.

Check out our website at **www.kensingtonbooks.com**

Put a Little Romance in Your Life With
Janelle Taylor

__Anything for Love	0-8217-4992-7	$5.99US/$6.99CAN
__Forever Ecstasy	0-8217-5241-3	$5.99US/$6.99CAN
__Fortune's Flames	0-8217-5450-5	$5.99US/$6.99CAN
__Destiny's Temptress	0-8217-5448-3	$5.99US/$6.99CAN
__Love Me With Fury	0-8217-5452-1	$5.99US/$6.99CAN
__First Love, Wild Love	0-8217-5277-4	$5.99US/$6.99CAN
__Kiss of the Night Wind	0-8217-5279-0	$5.99US/$6.99CAN
__Love With a Stranger	0-8217-5416-5	$6.99US/$8.50CAN
__Forbidden Ecstasy	0-8217-5278-2	$5.99US/$6.99CAN
__Defiant Ecstasy	0-8217-5447-5	$5.99US/$6.99CAN
__Follow the Wind	0-8217-5449-1	$5.99US/$6.99CAN
__Wild Winds	0-8217-6026-2	$6.99US/$8.50CAN
__Defiant Hearts	0-8217-5563-3	$6.50US/$8.00CAN
__Golden Torment	0-8217-5451-3	$5.99US/$6.99CAN
__Bittersweet Ecstasy	0-8217-5445-9	$5.99US/$6.99CAN
__Taking Chances	0-8217-4259-0	$4.50US/$5.50CAN
__By Candlelight	0-8217-5703-2	$6.99US/$8.50CAN
__Chase the Wind	0-8217-4740-1	$5.99US/$6.99CAN
__Destiny Mine	0-8217-5185-9	$5.99US/$6.99CAN
__Midnight Secrets	0-8217-5280-4	$5.99US/$6.99CAN
__Sweet Savage Heart	0-8217-5276-6	$5.99US/$6.99CAN
__Moonbeams and Magic	0-7860-0184-4	$5.99US/$6.99CAN
__Brazen Ecstasy	0-8217-5446-7	$5.99US/$6.99CAN

Call toll free **1-888-345-BOOK** to order by phone or use this coupon to order by mail.

Name _____

Address _____

City _____ State _____ Zip _____

Please send me the books I have checked above.

I am enclosing $_____
Plus postage and handling* $_____
Sales tax (in New York and Tennessee) $_____
Total amount enclosed $_____

*Add $2.50 for the first book and $.50 for each additional book.

Send check or money order (no cash or CODs) to:

Kensington Publishing Corp., 850 Third Avenue, New York, NY 10022

Prices and Numbers subject to change without notice.

All orders subject to availability.

Check out our website at **www.kensingtonbooks.com**

Put a Little Romance in Your Life With
Fern Michaels

__**Dear Emily**	0-8217-5676-1	$6.99US/$8.50CAN
__**Sara's Song**	0-8217-5856-X	$6.99US/$8.50CAN
__**Wish List**	0-8217-5228-6	$6.99US/$7.99CAN
__**Vegas Rich**	0-8217-5594-3	$6.99US/$8.50CAN
__**Vegas Heat**	0-8217-5758-X	$6.99US/$8.50CAN
__**Vegas Sunrise**	1-55817-5983-3	$6.99US/$8.50CAN
__**Whitefire**	0-8217-5638-9	$6.99US/$8.50CAN

Call toll free **1-888-345-BOOK** to order by phone or use this coupon to order by mail.

Name_____

Address_____

City _____ State _____Zip_____

Please send me the books I have checked above.

I am enclosing	$_____
Plus postage and handling*	$_____
Sales tax (in New York and Tennessee)	$_____
Total amount enclosed	$_____

*Add $2.50 for the first book and $.50 for each additional book.

Send check or money order (no cash or CODs) to:

Kensington Publishing Corp., 850 Third Avenue, New York, NY 10022

Prices and Numbers subject to change without notice.

All orders subject to availability.

Check out our website at **www.kensingtonbooks.com**

Put a Little Romance in Your Life With
Hannah Howell

__My Valiant Knight $5.50US/$7.00CAN
 0-8217-5186-7

__Only For You $5.99US/$7.50CAN
 0-8217-5943-4

__Unconquered $5.99US/$7.50CAN
 0-8217-5417-3

__Wild Roses $5.99US/$7.50CAN
 0-8217-5677-X

__Highland Destiny $5.99US/$7.50CAN
 0-8217-5921-3

__Highland Honor $5.99US/$7.50CAN
 0-8217-6095-5

__A Taste of Fire $5.99US/$7.50CAN
 0-8217-5804-7

Call toll free **1-888-345-BOOK** to order by phone or use this coupon to order by mail.

Name _____

Address _____

City _____ State _____ Zip _____

Please send me the books I have checked above.

I am enclosing $_____

Plus postage and handling* $_____

Sales tax (in New York and Tennessee) $_____

Total amount enclosed $_____

*Add $2.50 for the first book and $.50 for each additional book.

Send check or money order (no cash or CODs) to:

Kensington Publishing Corp., 850 Third Avenue, New York, NY 10022

Prices and Numbers subject to change without notice.

All orders subject to availability.

Check out our website at **www.kensingtonbooks.com**